"Well, honey, I can tell you for a fact that I have a little bit of dark that I carry around with me."

"I guess as long as we stay in the light it should be okay."

Levi was tempted to toy with her. He didn't know if she was being intentionally flirtatious. But there was something so open, so innocent about her expression, he doubted it.

"I'm going to go sketch," Faith said. "Now that I've seen the place, and you've sent over all the meaningful information, I should be able to come up with an initial draft. And then I can send it over to you."

"Sounds good," he said. "Then what?"

"Then we'll arrange another meeting."

"Sounds like a plan," he said, extending his hand. He shouldn't touch her again. But he wanted to.

Pink colored her cheeks. A blush.

Dammit all, the woman had blushed.

Women who blushed were not for men like him.

* * *

Need Me, Cowboy by *New York Times* bestselling author Maisey Yates is part of the Copper Ridge series.

MAISEY YATES

NEED ME, COWBOY

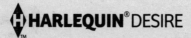

HARLEQUIN® DESIRE

Recycling programs
for this product may
not exist in your area.

ISBN-13: 978-1-335-60355-5

Need Me, Cowboy

Copyright © 2019 by Maisey Yates

Printed in U.S.A.

In Copper Ridge, Oregon, lasting love with a cowboy is only a happily-ever-after away. Don't miss any of **Maisey Yates**'s Copper Ridge tales, available now!

From Harlequin Desire

Take Me, Cowboy
Hold Me, Cowboy
Seduce Me, Cowboy
Claim Me, Cowboy
Want Me, Cowboy
Need Me, Cowboy

From HQN Books

Shoulda Been a Cowboy (prequel novella)
Part Time Cowboy
Brokedown Cowboy
Bad News Cowboy
A Copper Ridge Christmas (ebook novella)
The Cowboy Way
Hometown Heartbreaker (ebook novella)
One Night Charmer
Tough Luck Hero
Last Chance Rebel
Slow Burn Cowboy
Down Home Cowboy
Wild Ride Cowboy
Christmastime Cowboy

For more books by Maisey Yates,
visit maiseyyates.com.

Prologue

Levi Tucker
Oregon State Penitentiary
2605 State St., Salem, OR 97310

Dear Ms. Grayson,
Due to certain circumstances, my prison sentence is coming to its end sooner than originally scheduled. I've been following your career and I'd like to hire you to design the house I intend to have built.
Sincerely,
Levi Tucker

Dear Mr. Tucker,
How nice that you're soon to be released from prison. I imagine that's a great relief. As you

can imagine, my work is in very high demand and I doubt I'll be able to take on a project with such short notice.
Regretfully,
Faith Grayson

Dear Ms. Grayson,
Whatever your usual fee is, I can double it.
Sincerely,
Levi Tucker

Dear Mr. Tucker,
To be perfectly frank, I looked you up on Google. My brothers would take a dim view of me agreeing to take this job.
Respectfully,
Faith Grayson

Dear Ms. Grayson,
Search again. You'll find I am in the process of being exonerated. Also, what your brothers don't know won't hurt anything. I'll triple your fee.
Sincerely,
Levi Tucker

Dear Mr. Tucker,
If you need to contact me, be sure to use my personal number, listed at the bottom of this page.
I trust we'll be in contact upon your release.
Faith

One

Levi Tucker wasn't a murderer.

It was a fact that was now officially recognized by the law.

He didn't know what he had expected upon his release from prison. Relief, maybe. He imagined that was what most men might feel. Instead, the moment the doors to the penitentiary had closed behind him, Levi had felt something else.

A terrible, pure anger that burned through his veins with a kind of white-hot clarity that would have stunned him if it hadn't felt so inevitable.

The fact of the matter was, Levi Tucker had always known he wasn't a murderer.

And all the state of Oregon had ever had was a hint of suspicion. Hell, they hadn't even had a body.

Mostly because Alicia wasn't dead.

In many ways, that added insult to injury, because he still had to divorce the woman who had set out to make it look as though he had killed her. They were still married. Of course, the moment he'd been able to, he'd filed, and he knew everything was in the process of being sorted out.

He doubted she would contest.

But then, how could he really know?

He had thought he'd known the woman. Hell, he'd married her. And while he'd been well aware that everything hadn't been perfect, he had not expected his wife to disappear one hot summer night, leaving behind implications of foul play.

Even if the result hadn't been intentional, she could have resurfaced at any point after she'd disappeared.

When he was being questioned. When he had been arrested.

She hadn't.

Leaving him to assume that his arrest, disgrace and abject humiliation had been her goal.

It made him wonder now if their relationship had been a long-tail game all the time.

The girl who'd loved him in spite of his family's reputation in Copper Ridge. The one who'd vowed to stick with him through everything. No matter whether he made his fortune or not. He had, and he'd vowed to Alicia he'd build her a house on top of a hill in Copper Ridge so they could look down on all the people who'd once looked down on them.

But until then he'd enjoyed his time at work, away

from the town he'd grown up in. Alicia had gotten more involved in the glamorous side of their new lifestyle, while Levi just wanted things to be simple. His own ranch. His own horses.

Alicia had wanted more.

And apparently, in the end, she had figured she could have it all without him.

Fortunately, it was the money that had ultimately been her undoing. For years prior to her leaving she'd been siphoning it into her own account without him realizing it, but when her funds had run dry she'd gone after the money still in his accounts. And that was when she'd gotten caught.

She'd been living off of his hard-earned money for years.

Five years.

Five hellish years he'd spent locked up as the murderer of a woman. Of his wife.

Not a great situation, all in all.

But he'd survived it. Like he'd survived every damn thing that had come before it.

Money was supposed to protect you.

In the end, he supposed it had, in many ways.

Hell, he might not have been able to walk out of that jail cell and collect his Stetson on his way back to his life if it wasn't for the fact that he had a good team of lawyers who had gotten his case retried as quickly as possible. Something you would've thought would be pretty easy considering his wife had been found alive.

The boy he'd been…

He had no confidence that boy would have been able to get justice.

But the man he was...

The man he was now stood on a vacant plot of land that he owned, near enough to the house he was renting, and waited for the architect to arrive. The one who would design the house he deserved after spending five years behind bars.

There would be no bars in this house. The house that Alicia had wanted so badly. To show everyone in their hometown that he and Alicia were more, were better, than what they'd been born into.

Only, she wasn't.

Without him, she was nothing. And he would prove that to her.

No, his house would have no bars. Nothing but windows.

Windows with a view of the mountains that over-looked Copper Ridge, Oregon, the town where he had grown up. He'd been bad news back then; his whole family had been.

The kind of guy that fathers warned their daughters about.

A bad seed dropped from a rotten tree.

And he had a feeling that public opinion would not have changed in the years since.

His reputation certainly hadn't helped his case when he'd been tried and convicted five years ago.

Repeating patterns. That had been brought up many times. An abusive father was likely to have raised an abusive son, who had gone on to be a murderer.

That was the natural progression, wasn't it?

The natural progression of men like him.

Alicia had known that. Of course she had. She knew him better than any other person on earth.

Yet he hadn't known her at all.

Well, he had ended up in prison, as she'd most likely intended. But he'd clawed his way out. And now he was going to stand up on the mountain in his fancy-ass house and look down on everyone who'd thought prison would be the end of him.

The best house in the most prime location in town. That was his aim.

Now all that was left to do was wait for Faith Grayson to arrive. By all accounts she was the premier architect at the moment, the hottest commodity in custom home design.

Her houses were more than simple buildings, they were works of art. And he was bound and determined to own a piece of that art for himself.

He was a man possessed. A man on a mission to make the most of everything he'd lost. To live as well as possible while his wife had to deal with the slow-rolling realization that she would be left with nothing.

As it was, it was impossible to prove that she had committed a crime. She hadn't called the police, after all. An argument could be made that she might *not* have intended for him to be arrested. And there was plausible deniability over the fact that she might not have realized he'd gone to prison.

She claimed she had simply walked away from her life and not looked back. The fact that she had been accessing money was a necessity, so she said. And proof that she had not actually been attempting to hide.

He didn't believe that. He didn't believe *her*, and she had been left with nothing. No access to his money at all. She had been forced to go crawling back to her parents to get an allowance. And he was glad of that.

They said the best revenge was living well.

Levi Tucker intended to do just that.

Faith Grayson knew that meeting an ex-convict at the top of an isolated mountain could easily be filed directly into the Looney Tunes Bin.

Except, Levi Tucker was only an ex-convict because he had been wrongfully convicted in the first place. At least, that was the official statement from the Oregon State District Attorney's office.

Well, plus it was obvious because his wife wasn't dead.

He had been convicted of the murder of someone who was alive. And while there was a whole lot of speculation centered around the fact that the woman never would have run from him in the first place if he hadn't been dangerous and terrifying, the fact remained that he *wasn't* a killer.

So, there was that.

She knew exactly what two of her brothers, Isaiah and Joshua, would say about this meeting. And it would be colorful. Not at all supportive.

But Faith was fascinated by the man who was willing to pay so much to get one of her designs. And maybe her ego was a little bit turbocharged by the whole thing. She couldn't deny that.

She was only human, after all.

A human who had been working really, really hard to keep on top of her status as a rising star in the architecture world.

She had designed buildings that had changed skylines, and she'd done homes for the rich and the famous.

Levi Tucker was something *else*. He was infamous.

The self-made millionaire whose whole world had come crashing down when his wife had disappeared more than five years ago. The man who had been tried and convicted of her murder even when there wasn't a body.

Who had spent the past five years in prison, and who was now digging his way back out...

He wanted her. And yeah, it interested her.

She was getting bored.

Which seemed...ungrateful. Her skill for design had made her famous at a ridiculously young age, but, of course, it was her older brothers and their business acumen that had helped her find success so quickly.

Joshua was a public-relations wizard, Isaiah a genius with finance. Faith, for her part, was the one with the imagination.

The one who saw buildings growing out of the ground like trees and worked to find ways to twist them into new shapes, to draw new lines into the man-made landscape to blend it all together with nature.

She had always been an artist, but her fascination with buildings had come from a trip her family had taken when she was a child. They had driven from Copper Ridge into Portland, Oregon, and she had been struck by the beauty that surrounded the city.

But in the part of the city where they'd stayed, everything was blocky and made of concrete. Of course, there were parts of the city that were lovely, with architecture that was ornate and classic, but there were parts where the buildings had been stacked in light gray rectangles, and it had nearly wounded her to see the mountains obscured by such unimaginative, dull shapes.

When she had gotten back to their hotel room, she had begun to draw, trying to find a way to blend function and form with the natural beauty that already existed.

It had become an obsession.

It was tough to be an obsessed person. Someone who lived in their own head, in their dreams and fantasies.

It made it difficult to relate to people.

Fortunately, she had found a good friend, Mia,

who had been completely understanding of Faith and her particular idiosyncrasies.

Now Mia was her sister-in-law, because she had married Faith's oldest brother, something Faith really hadn't seen coming.

Devlin was just…so much older. There was more than ten years between him and Faith, and she'd had no idea her friend felt that way about him.

She was happy for both of them, of course.

But their bond sometimes made her feel isolated. The fact that her friend now had this *thing* that Faith herself never had. And that this *thing* was with Faith's brother. Of all people.

Even Joshua and Isaiah had fallen in love and gotten married.

Joshua had wed a woman he had met while trying to get revenge on their father for attempting to force him into marriage, while Isaiah married his personal assistant.

Maybe it was her family that had driven Faith to the top of the mountain today.

Maybe her dissatisfaction with her own personal life was why it felt so interesting and new to do something with Levi Tucker.

Everything she had accomplished, she had done with the permission and help of other people.

If she was going to be a visionary, she wanted—just this once—for it to be on her terms.

To not be seen as a child prodigy—which was ridiculous, because she was twenty-five, not a child at all—but to be seen as someone who was really great at what she did. To leave her age out of it, to leave her older brothers—who often felt more like babysitters—out of it.

She let out a long, slow breath as she rounded the final curve on the mountain driveway, the vacant lot coming into view. But it wasn't the lot, or the scenery surrounding it, that stood out in her vision first and foremost. No, it was the man standing there, his hands shoved into the pockets of his battered jeans, worn cowboy boots on his feet. He had on a black T-shirt, in spite of the morning chill, and a black cowboy hat was pressed firmly onto his head.

Both of his arms were completely filled with ink, the dark lines of the tattoos painting pictures on his skin she couldn't quite see from where she was.

But in a strange way, they reminded her of architecture. The tattoos seemed to enhance the muscle there, to draw focus to the skin beneath the lines, even while they covered it.

She parked the car and sat for a moment, completely struck dumb by the sight of him.

She had researched him, obviously. She knew what he looked like, but she supposed she hadn't had a sense of…the scale of him.

Strange, because she was usually pretty good at picking up on those kinds of things in photographs. She had a mathematical eye, one that blended with her artistic sensibility in a way that felt natural to her.

And yet, she had not been able to accurately form a picture of the man in her mind. And when she got out of the car, she was struck by the way he seemed to fill this vast empty space.

That also didn't make any sense.

He was big. Over six feet and with broad shoulders, but he didn't fill this space. Not literally.

But she could feel his presence like a touch as soon as the cold air wrapped itself around her body upon exiting the car.

And when his ice-blue eyes connected with hers, she drew in a breath. She was certain he filled her lungs, too.

Because that air no longer felt cold. It felt hot. Impossibly so.

Because those blue eyes burned with something.

Rage. Anger.

Not at her—in fact, his expression seemed almost friendly.

But there was something simmering beneath the surface, and it had touched her already.

Wouldn't let go of her.

"Ms. Grayson," he said, his voice rolling over her with that same kind of heat. "Good to meet you."

He stuck out his hand and she hurriedly closed the distance between them, flinching before their skin touched, because she knew it was going to burn.

It did.

"Mr. Tucker," she responded, careful to keep her voice neutral, careful when she released her hold on him, not to flex her fingers or wipe her palm against the side of her skirt like she wanted to.

"This is the site," he said. "I hope you think it's workable."

"I do," she said, blinking. She needed to look around them. At the view. At the way the house would be situated. This lot was more than usable. It was inspirational. "What do you have in mind? I find it best to begin with customer expectations," she said, quick to turn the topic where it needed to go. Because what she didn't want to do was ponder the man any longer.

The man didn't matter.

The house mattered.

"I want it to be everything prison isn't," he said, his tone hard and decisive.

She couldn't imagine this man, as vast and wild as the deep green trees and ridged blue mountains around them, contained in a cell. Isolated. Cut off.

In darkness.

And suddenly she felt compelled to be the answer to that darkness. To make sure that the walls she built for him didn't feel like walls at all.

"Windows," she said. That was the easiest and most obvious thing. A sense of openness and free-dom. She began to plot the ways in which she could construct a house so that it didn't have doors. So that things were concealed by angles and curves. "No doors?"

"I live alone," he said simply. "There's no reason for doors."

"And you don't plan on living with someone any-time soon?"

"Never," he responded. "It may surprise you to learn that I have cooled on the idea of marriage."

"Windows. Lighting." She turned to the east. "The sun should be up here early, and we can try to capture the light there in the morning when you wake up, and then…" She turned the opposite way. "Make sure that we're set up for you to see the light as it goes down here. Kitchen. Living room. Office?"

Her fingers twitched and she pulled her sketch pad out of her large leather bag, jotting notes and rough lines as quickly as possible. She felt the skin prickle on her face and she paused, looking up.

He was watching her.

She cleared her throat. "Can I ask you…what was it that inspired you to get in touch with me? Which building of mine?"

"All of them," he said. "I had nothing but time while I was in jail, and while I did what I could to manage some of my assets from behind bars, there was a lot of time to read. An article about your achievements came to my attention and I was fascinated by your work. I won't lie to you—even more than that, I am looking forward to owning a piece of you."

Something about those words hit her square in the solar plexus and radiated outward. She was sweating now. She was not wearing her coat. She should not be sweating.

"Of me?"

"Your brand," he said. "Having a place designed by you is an exceedingly coveted prize, I believe."

She felt her cheeks warm, and she couldn't quite figure out why. She didn't suffer from false modesty. The last few years of her life had been nothing short of extraordinary. She embraced her success and she didn't apologize for it. Didn't duck her head, like she was doing now, or tuck her hair behind her ear and look up bashfully. Which she had just done.

"I suppose so."

"You know it's true," he said.

"Yes," she said, clearing her throat and rallying. "I do."

"Whatever the media might say, whatever law enforcement believes now, my wife tried to destroy my life. And I will not allow her to claim that victory. I'm not a phoenix rising from the ashes. I'm just a very angry man ready to set some shit on fire, and stand there watching it burn. I'm going to show her, and the world, that I can't be destroyed. I'm not slinking into the shadows. I'm going to rebuild it all. Until everything that I have done matters more than what she did to me. I will not allow her name, what she did, to be the thing I am remembered for. I'm sure you can understand that."

She could. Oddly, she really could.

She wasn't angry at anyone, nor did she have any right to be, but she knew what it was like to want to break out and have your own achievements. Wasn't that what she had just been thinking of while coming here?

Of course, he already had so many achievements.

She imagined having all her work blotted out the way that he had. It was unacceptable.

"Look," she said, stashing her notebook, "I meant what I said, about my brothers being unhappy with me for taking this job."

"What do your brothers have to do with you taking a job?"

"If you read anything about me then you know that I work with them. You know that we've merged with the construction company that handles a great deal of our building."

"Yes, I know. Though, doesn't the construction arm mostly produce reproductions of your designs, rather than handling your custom projects?"

"It depends," she responded. "I just mean… My brothers run a significant portion of our business."

"But you could go off and run it without them. They can't run it without you."

He had said the words she had thought more than once while listening to Joshua and Isaiah make proclamations about various things. Joshua was charming, and often managed to make his proclamations seem not quite so prescriptive. Isaiah never bothered. About the only person he was soft with at all was his wife, Poppy, who owned his heart—a heart that a great many of them had doubted he had.

"Well, I just meant… We need to keep this project a secret. Until we're at least most of the way through. Jonathan Bear will be the one to handle the building. He's the best. And since you're right here in Copper Ridge, it would make sense to have him do it."

"I know Jonathan Bear," Levi said.

That surprised her. "Do you?"

"I'm a couple years older than him, but we both grew up on the same side of the tracks here in town. You know, the wrong side."

"Oh," she said. "I didn't realize."

Dimly, she had been aware, on some level, that Levi was from here, but he had left so long ago, and he was so far outside of her own peer group that she would never have known him.

If he was older than Jonathan Bear, then he was possibly a good thirteen years her senior.

That made her feel small and silly for that instant response she'd had to him earlier.

She was basically a child to him.

But then, she was basically a child to most of the men in her life, so why should this be any different?

And she didn't even know why it was bothering her.

She often designed buildings for old men. And in the beginning, it had been difficult getting them to take her seriously, but the more pieces that had been written about her, the more those men had marveled at the talent she had for her age, and the more she was able to walk into a room with all of those accolades clearly visible behind her as she went.

She was still a little bit bothered that her age was such a big deal, but if it helped…then she would take it. Because she couldn't do anything about the fact that she looked like she might still be in college.

She tried—*tried*—to affect a sophisticated appearance, but half the time she felt like she was playing dress-up in a much fancier woman's clothes.

"Clandestine architecture project?" he asked, the corner of his lips working up into a smile. And until that moment, she realized she had not been fully convinced his mouth could do that.

"Something like that."

"Let me ask you this," he said. "Why do you want to take the job?"

"Well, it's like you said. I—I feel like I'm an important piece of the business. And believe me, I wouldn't be where I am without Isaiah and Joshua. They're brilliant. But I want to be able to make my own choices. Maybe I want to take on this project. Especially now that you've said…everything about needing it to be the opposite of a prison cell. I'm inspired to do it. I love this location. I want to build this house without Isaiah hovering over me."

Levi chuckled, low and gravelly. "So he wouldn't approve of me?"

"Not at all."

"I am innocent," he said. His mouth worked upward again. "Or I should say, I'm not guilty. Whether or not I'm an entirely innocent person is another story. But I didn't do anything to my wife."

"Your ex-wife?"

"Nearly. Everything should be finalized in the next couple of days. She's not contesting anything. Mostly because she doesn't want to end up in prison. I have impressed upon her how unpleasant that experience was. She has no desire to see for herself."

"Oh, of course you're still married to her. Because everybody thought—"

"That she was dead. You don't have to divorce a dead person."

"Let me ask you something," she said, doing her best to meet his gaze, ignoring the quivering sensation she felt in her belly. "Do I have reason to be afraid of you?"

The grin that spread over his face was slow, calculated. "Well, I would say that depends."

Two

He shouldn't toy with her. It wasn't nice. But then, he wasn't nice. He hadn't been, not even before his stint in prison. But the time there had taken anything soft inside of him and hardened it. Until his insides were a minefield of sharpened obsidian. Black, stone-cold, honed into a razor.

The man he'd been before might not have done anything to provoke the pretty little woman in front of him. But he could barely remember that man. That man had been an idiot. That man had married Alicia, had convinced himself he could have a happy life, when he had never seen any kind of happiness come from marriage, not all through his childhood. So why had he thought he could have more? Could have something else?

"Depends on what?" she asked, looking up at him,

those wide brown eyes striking him square in the chest…and lower, when they made contact with his.

She was so very pretty.

So very young, too.

Her pale, heart-shaped face, those soft-looking pink lips and her riot of brown curls—it all appealed to him in an instant, visceral way.

No real mystery, he supposed. He hadn't touched a woman in more than five years.

This one was contraband. She had a use, but it wouldn't be *that* one.

Hell, no.

He was a hard bastard, no mistake. But he wasn't a criminal.

He didn't belong with the rapists and murderers he'd been locked away with for all those years, and sometimes the only thing that had kept him going in those subhuman conditions—where he'd been called every name in the book, subjected to threats that would make most men weep with fear in their beds—was the knowledge that he didn't belong there.

That he wasn't one of them.

Hell, that was about the only thing that had kept him from hunting down Alicia when he'd been released.

He wasn't a murderer. He wasn't a monster.

He wouldn't let Alicia make him one.

"Depends on what scares you," he said.

She firmed those full lips into a thin, ungenerous line, and perhaps that reaction should have turned his thoughts in a different direction.

Instead he thought about what it might take to coax those lips back to softness. To fullness. And just how much riper they might become if he was to kiss them. To take the lower one between his teeth and bite.

He really wasn't fit for company. At least not delicate, female company.

Sadly, it was delicate female company that seemed appealing.

He needed to go to a bar and find a woman more like him. Harder. Closer to his age.

Someone who could stand five years of pent-up sexual energy pounded into her body.

The sweet little architect he had hired was not that woman.

If her brothers had any idea she was meeting with him they would get out their pitchforks. If they had any idea what he was thinking now, they would get out their shotguns.

And he couldn't blame them.

"Spiders. Do you have spiders up your sleeves?"

"No spiders," he said.

"The dark?"

"Well, honey, I can tell you for a fact that I have a little bit of that I carry around with me."

"I guess as long as we stay in the light it should be okay."

He was tempted to toy with her. He didn't know if she was being intentionally flirtatious. But there was something so open, so innocent, about her expression that he doubted it.

"I'm going to go sketch," she said. "Now that I've seen the place, and you've sent over all the meaningful information, I should be able to come up with an initial draft. And then I can send it over to you."

"Sounds good," he said. "Then what?"

"Then we'll arrange another meeting."

"Sounds like a plan," he said, extending his hand.

He shouldn't touch her again. When her soft fingers had closed around his he had felt that around his cock.

But he wanted to touch her again.

Pink colored her cheeks. A blush.

Dammit all, the woman had blushed.

Women who blushed were not for men like him.

That he had a sense of that at all was a reminder. A reminder that he wasn't an animal. Wasn't a monster.

Or at least that he still had enough man in him to control himself.

"I'll see you then."

Three

Faith was not hugely conversant in the whole girls'-night-out thing. Mia, her best friend from school, was not big on going out, and never had been, and usually, that had suited Faith just fine.

Faith had been a scholarship student at a boarding school that would have been entirely out of her family's reach if the school hadn't been interested in her artistic talents. And she'd been so invested in making the most of those talents, and then making the most of her scholarships in college, that she'd never really made time to go out.

And Mia had always been much the same, so there had been no one to encourage the other one to go out.

After school it had been work. Work and more work, and riding the massive wave Faith had somehow managed to catch that had buoyed her career to nearly absurd levels as soon as she'd graduated.

But since coming to Copper Ridge, things had somehow managed to pick up and slow down at the same time. There was something about living in a small town, with its slower pace, clean streets and wide-open spaces all around, that seemed to create more time.

Not having to commute through Seattle traffic helped, and it might actually be the sum total of where she had found all that extra time, if she was honest.

She had also begun to make friends with Hayley Bear, formerly Thompson, now wife of Jonathan. When Faith and her brothers had moved their head-quarters to Copper Ridge, closer to their parents, Joshua had decided it would be a good idea to find a local builder to partner with, and that was how they'd met Jonathan and merged their businesses.

And tonight, Faith and Hayley were out for drinks.

Of course, Hayley didn't really drink, and Faith was a lightweight at best, but that didn't mean they couldn't have fun.

They were also in Hayley's brother's bar.

They couldn't have been supervised any better if they'd tried. Though, the protectiveness was going to be directed more at Hayley than Faith.

Faith stuck her straw down deep into her rum and Coke and fished out a cherry, lifting it up and chewing it thoughtfully as she surveyed the room.

The revelers were out in force, whole groups of cheering friends standing by Ferdinand, the mechanical bull, and watching as people stepped up to the plate—both drunk and sober—to get thrown off his back and onto the mats below.

It looked entirely objectionable to Faith. She couldn't imagine submitting herself to something like that. A ride you couldn't control, couldn't anticipate. Where the only way off was to weather the bucking or get thrown to the mats below.

No, thanks.

"You seem quiet," Hayley pointed out.

"Do I?" Faith mused.

"Yes," Hayley said. "You seem like you have something on your mind."

Faith gnawed the inside of her cheek. "I'm starting a new design project. And it's really important that I get everything right. I mean, I'm going to be collaborating with the guy, so I'm sure he'll have his own input, and all of that, but…" She didn't know how to explain it without giving herself away, then she gave up. "If I told you something…could you keep it a secret?"

Hayley blinked her wide brown eyes. "Yes. Though… I don't keep anything from Jonathan. Ever. He's my husband and…"

"Can Jonathan keep a secret?"

"Jonathan doesn't really do…*friends*. So, I'm not sure who he would tell. I think I might be the only person he talks to."

"He works with my brothers," Faith pointed out.

"To the same degree he works with you."

"Not really. A lot more of the stuff filters through Joshua and Isaiah than it does me. I'm just kind of around. That's our agreement. They handle all of the…business stuff. And I do the drawing. The designing. I'm an expert at buildings and building materials, aesthetics and design. Not so much anything else."

"Point taken. But, yes, if I asked Jonathan not to say something, he wouldn't. He's totally loyal to me." Hayley looked a little bit smug about that.

It was hard to have friends who were so happily… *relationshipped*, when Faith knew so little about how that worked.

Though at least Hayley wasn't with Faith's *brother*.

Yes, that made Faith and Mia family, which was nice in its way, but it really limited their ability to talk about boys. They had always promised to share personal things, like first times. While Faith had been happy for her friend, and for her brother, she also had wanted details about as much as she wanted to be stripped naked, have a string tied around her toe and be dragged through the small town's main street by her brother Devlin's Harley.

As in: not at all.

"I took a job that Joshua and Isaiah are going to be really mad about…"

Just then, the door to the bar opened, and Faith's

mouth dropped open. Because there he was. Speaking of.

Hayley looked over her shoulder, not bothering to be subtle. "Who's that?" she hissed.

"The devil," Faith said softly.

Hayley blinked. "You had better start at the beginning."

"I was about to," Faith said.

The two of them watched as Levi went up to the counter, leaned over and placed an order with Ace, the bartender and owner of the bar, and Hayley's older brother.

"That's Levi Tucker," Faith said.

Hayley narrowed her eyes. "Why do I know that name?"

"Because he's kind of famous. Like, a famous murderer."

"Oh, my gosh," Hayley said, slapping the table with her open palm, "he's that guy. That guy accused of murdering his wife! But she wasn't really dead."

"Yes," Faith confirmed.

"You're working with him?"

"I'm designing a house for him. But he's not a murderer. Yes, he was in prison for a while, but he didn't actually do anything. His wife disappeared. That's not exactly his fault."

Hayley looked at Faith skeptically. "If I ran away from my husband it would have to be for a pretty extreme reason."

"Well, no one's ever proven that he did anything.

And, anyway, I'm just working with him in a professional capacity. I'm not scared of him."

"Should you be?"

Faith took in the long, hard lines of his body, the dark tattoos on his arms, that dark cowboy hat pulled low over his eyes and his sculpted jaw, which she imagined a woman could cut her hand on if she caressed it…

"No," she said quickly. "Why would I need to be scared of him? I'm designing a house for the guy. Nothing else."

He began to scan the room, and she felt the sudden urge to hide from that piercing blue gaze. Her heart was thundering like she had just run a marathon. Like she just might actually be…

Afraid.

No. That was silly. Impossible. There really wasn't anything to be afraid of.

He was just a man. A hard, scarred man with ink all over his skin, but that didn't mean he was bad. Or scary.

Devlin had tattoos over every visible inch of his body from the neck down.

She didn't want to know if they were anywhere else. There were just some things you shouldn't know about your brother.

But yeah, tattoos didn't make a man scary. Or dangerous. She knew that.

So she couldn't figure out why her heart was still racing.

And then he saw them.

She felt a rush of heat move over her body as he raised his hand and gripped the brim of his cowboy hat, tipping his head down slowly in a brief acknowledgment.

She swallowed hard, her throat sticky and dry, then reached for her soda, feeling panicky. She took a long sip, forgetting there was rum in it, the burn making her cough.

"This is concerning," Hayley said softly, her expression overly sharp.

"What is?" Faith asked, jerking her gaze away from Levi.

"You're *not* acting normal."

"I'm not used to subterfuge." Faith sounded defensive. Because she felt a little defensive.

"The look on your face has nothing to do with the fact that he's incredibly attractive?"

"Is he?" Faith asked, her tone disingenuous, but sweet. "I hadn't noticed."

Actually, until Hayley had said that, she hadn't noticed. Well, she had, but she hadn't connected that disquiet in her stomach with finding him…*attractive*.

He was out of her league in every way. Too old for her. Too hard for her.

Levi was the deep end of the pool, and she didn't know how to swim. That much, she knew.

And she wouldn't… He was a client. Even if she was a champion lap swimmer, there was no way.

He was no longer acknowledging her or Hayley, anyway, as his focus turned back to the bar.

"What's going on with you?" Faith asked, very clumsily changing the subject and forcing herself to look at Hayley.

She and Hayley began to chat about other things, and she did her best to forget that Levi Tucker was in the bar at all.

He had obviously forgotten she was there, anyway.

Then, for some reason, some movement caught her attention, and she turned.

Levi was talking to a blonde, his head bent low, a smile on his face that made Faith feel like she'd just heard him say a dirty word. The blonde was looking back at him with the exact same expression. She was wearing a top that exposed her midriff, which was tight and tan, with a little sparkling piercing on her stomach.

She was exactly the kind of woman Faith could never hope to be, or compete with. And she shouldn't want to, anyway.

Obviously, Levi Tucker was at the bar looking for a good time. And Faith wasn't going to be the one to give it to him, so Blondie McBellyRing might as well be the one to do it.

It was no skin off Faith's nose.

Right then, Levi looked up, and his ice-blue gaze collided with hers with the force of an iceberg hitting the *Titanic*.

And damn if she didn't feel like she was sinking.

He put his hand on the blonde's hip, leaning in and saying something to her, patting her gently before moving away…and walking straight in Faith's direction.

Four

Levi had no idea what in the hell he was doing.

He was chatting up Mindy—who was a sure thing if there ever was one—and close to breaking that dry spell. He'd watched the little blonde ride that mechanical bull like an expert, and he figured she was exactly the kind of woman who could stay on his rough ride for as long as he needed her to.

A few minutes of banter had confirmed that, and he'd been ready to close the deal.

But then he'd caught Faith Grayson staring at them. And now, for no reason he could discern, he was on his way over to Faith.

Because it was weird he hadn't greeted her with more than just a hat tip from across the room, he told himself, as he crossed the rough-hewn wood floor and moved closer to her.

And not for any other reason.

"Fancy meeting you here," he said, ignoring the intent look he was getting from Faith's friend.

"Small towns," Faith said, shrugging and looking like she was ready to fold in on herself.

"You're used to them, aren't you? Aren't you originally from Copper Ridge?"

She nodded. "Yes. But until recently, I haven't lived here since I was seventeen."

"I'm going to get a refill," her friend announced suddenly, sliding out of her seat and making her way over to the bar.

Faith was looking after her friend like she wanted to punch the other woman. It made him wonder what he'd missed.

"She leaving you to get picked up on?" he asked, snagging the vacant seat beside her, his shoulder brushing hers.

She went stiff.

"No," Faith said, lowering her head, her cheeks turning an intense shade of pink.

Another reminder.

Another reminder he should go back over and talk to Mindy.

Faith was *young*. She blushed. She went rigid like a nervous jackrabbit when their shoulders touched. He didn't have the patience for that. He didn't want a woman who had to be shown what to do, even if he didn't mind the idea of corrupting her.

That thought immediately brought a kick of arousal straight to his gut.

All right, maybe his body didn't hate the idea of corrupting her. But he was in control of himself, and whatever baser impulses might exist inside of him, he had the final say.

"She vacated awfully quickly."

"That's Jonathan Bear's wife," she said conversationally, as if that was relevant to the conversation.

Well, it might not be relevant. But it was interesting.

His eyebrows shot up, and he looked back over at the pretty brunette, who was now standing at the counter chatting with the bartender. "And that's her brother," Faith continued.

"I didn't pick Jonathan Bear for a family man."

"He wasn't," Faith said. "Until he met Hayley."

Hayley was young. Not as young as Faith, but young. And Jonathan wasn't as old as Levi was.

That wasn't relevant, either.

"I haven't been to the bar since it changed ownership. Last I was here was…twenty years ago."

"How old are you?"

"Thirty-eight. I had a fake ID."

She laughed. "I didn't expect that."

"What? That I'm thirty-eight or that I had a fake ID?"

"Either."

Her pink tongue darted out and swept across her lips, leaving them wet and inviting. Then she looked down again, taking a sip of whatever it was in her glass. He wondered if she had any idea what she was doing. Just how inviting she'd made her mouth look.

Just how starving he was.

How willing he would be to devour her.

He looked back at Mindy, who was watching him with open curiosity. She didn't seem angry or jealous, just watching to see how her night was going to go, he imagined.

And that was exactly the kind of woman he should be talking to.

He was still rooted to the spot, though. And he didn't make a move back toward her.

"Are you going to be too hungover after tonight to come over to my place and discuss your plans?"

She looked behind him, directly at Mindy. "I figure I should ask you the same question."

"I'm betting I have a lot more hard-drinking years behind me than you do."

"I'm twenty-five," she said. Like that meant something.

"Oh, nothing to worry about, then."

"Four whole years of drinking," she said.

"Did you actually wait to drink until you were twenty-one?"

She blinked. "Yes."

"You know most people don't."

"That can't be true."

He didn't bother to hold in his laugh. "It is."

"I'm sure the…" She frowned. "I was about to say that I'm sure my brothers did. But… I bet they didn't."

She looked comically shocked by that. Who was this girl? This girl who had been lauded as a genius in a hundred articles, and designed the most amazing homes and buildings he'd ever seen. And seemed to know nothing about people.

"You know the deal about the Easter Bunny, too, right?" he asked.

She twisted her lips to the side. "That he has a very fluffy tail?"

He chuckled. "Yeah. That one."

He didn't know why it was difficult to pull himself away. It shouldn't be.

Dammit all, it shouldn't be.

"How about we meet up after lunch?" he asked, pushing the subject back to the house.

"That sounds good to me," she said, her tone a little bit breathless.

"You have the address where I'm staying?"

"Text it to me."

"I will."

He stood and walked away from her then, headed back toward the woman who would have been his conquest. He had another drink with Mindy, continuing to talk to her while she patted his arm, her movements flirtatious, her body language making it clear she was more than ready to have a good time. And for some reason, his body, which had been game a few moments earlier, wasn't all that interested anymore. He looked back over to where Faith and her friend had been sitting, and saw that the table was empty now.

He didn't know when she had left, and she hadn't bothered to say goodbye to him.

"You know what?" he said to Mindy. "I actually have work tomorrow."

She frowned. "Then why did you come out?"

"That's a good damn question." He tipped back his drink the rest of the way, committed now to getting a cab, because he was getting close to tipsy. "I'll make it up to you some other time."

She shrugged. "Well, I'm not going home. Tonight might not be a loss for me. Enjoy your right hand, honey."

If only she knew that even his right hand was a luxury. In shared living quarters with all the stuff that went down in prison, he'd never had the spare moment or the desire to beat off.

There was shame, and then there was the humiliation of finding a quiet corner in the dirty cell you shared with one or two other men.

No, thank you.

He would rather cut off his right hand than use it to add to all that BS.

It was better to just close off that part of himself. And he'd done it. Pretty damn effectively. He'd also managed to keep himself safe from all manner of prison violence that went on by building himself a rather ruthless reputation.

He had become a man who felt nothing. Certainly not pleasure or desire. A man who had learned to lash out before anyone could come at him.

The truly astonishing thing was how easy that had been.

How easy it had been to find that piece of his father that had probably lived inside of him all along.

"Maybe I will," he responded.

"So, are you really working early?" Mindy asked. "Or are you intent on joining that little brunette you were talking to earlier?"

Fire ignited in his gut.

"It'll be whatever I decide," he said, tipping his hat. "Have a good evening."

He walked out of the bar with his own words ringing in his head.

It would be what he would decide.

No one else had control over his life. Not now. Not ever.

Not anymore.

Five

The next morning, Faith's body was still teeming with weird emotions. It was difficult to untangle everything she was feeling. From what had begun when Hayley had called him attractive, to what she'd felt when she'd watched him continue to chat with the blonde, to when she had ultimately excused herself because she couldn't keep looking at their flirtation.

She realized—when she had been lying in her bed—that the reason she had to cut her girls' night short was that she couldn't stand knowing whether or not Levi left the bar with the pretty blonde.

She was sure he had. Why wouldn't he? He was a healthy, adult man. The kind who had apparently had a fake ID, so very likely a bad-boy type. Meaning that an impromptu one-night stand probably wouldn't bother him at all.

Heck, it had probably been why he was at the bar.

Her stomach felt like acid by the time she walked into the GrayBear Construction building.

The acidic feeling didn't improve when she saw that Joshua was already sitting there drinking a cup of coffee in the waiting room.

"What are you doing here?" she asked, then kicked the door shut with her foot and made her way over to the coffeemaker.

"Good morning."

"Shouldn't you be home having breakfast with your wife and kids?"

"I would be, but Danielle has an OB appointment later this morning." Joshua's wife was pregnant, and he was ridiculously happy about it. And Faith was happy for him. Two of her sisters-in-law were currently pregnant. Danielle very newly so, and Poppy due soon. Mia and Devlin seemed content to just enjoy each other for now.

Her brothers were happy. Faith was happy for them.

It was weird to be the last one so resolutely single, though. Even with her dating life so inactive, she had never imagined she would be the last single sibling in her family.

"I need to be at the appointment," he said. "She's getting an ultrasound."

"I see. So you came here to get work done early?"

"I've been here since six."

"I guess I can't scowl at you for that."

"Why are you scowling at all?"

She didn't say anything, and instead, she checked her buzzing text. It was from Levi. Just his address. Nothing more. It was awfully early. If he had a late night, would he be up texting her?

Maybe he's just still up.

She wanted to snarl at that little inner voice.

"You busy today?" Joshua asked casually.

"Not really. I have some schematics to go over. Some designs to do. Emails to send." She waved a hand. "A meeting later."

He frowned. "I don't have you down for a meeting."

Great. She should have known her PR brother would want to know what meeting she would be going out for.

"It's not, like, a work meeting. It's, like, for...a school talk." She stumbled over the lie, and immediately felt guilty.

"No school contacted me. Everything is supposed to go through me."

"I can handle community work in the town of Copper Ridge, Joshua. It's not like this is Seattle. And there's not going to be press anywhere asking me stupid questions or trying to trip me up. It's just Copper Ridge."

"Still."

The door opened and Isaiah came in, followed by his wife, Poppy, who was looking radiant in a tight, knee-length dress that showed off the full curve of her rounded stomach. They were holding hands, with their fingers laced together, and the contrast in their skin tones was beautiful—it always ignited a sense of artistic pleasure in Faith whenever she saw them. Well, and in general, seeing Isaiah happy made her feel that way. He was a difficult guy. Hard to understand, and seemingly emotionless sometimes.

But when he looked at Poppy... There was no doubt he was in love.

And no doubt that his wife was in love right back.

"Good morning," Isaiah said.

"Did you know Faith had a meeting with one of the schools today to give some kind of community-service talk?" Joshua launched right in. The dickhead.

"No," Isaiah said, looking at her. "You really need to clear these things with us."

"Why?"

"That's not on my schedule," Poppy said, pulling out her phone and poking around the screen.

"Don't start acting like my brothers," Faith said to her sister-in-law.

"It's my job to keep track of things," Poppy insisted.

"This is off the books," Faith said. "I'm allowed to have something that's just me. I'm an adult."

"You're young," Joshua said. "You're incredibly successful. Everyone wants a piece of that, and you can't afford to give out endless pieces of yourself."

She huffed and took a drink of her coffee. "I can manage, Joshua. I don't need you being controlling like this."

"The company functions in a specific way—"

"But my life doesn't. I don't need to give you an accounting of everything I do with my time. And not everything is work-related."

She spun on her heel and walked down the hall and, for some reason, was immediately hit with a flashback from last night. Levi didn't talk to her like she was a child. Levi almost…flirted with her. That was what last night had been like. Like flirting.

The idea gave her a little thrill.

But there was no way Levi had been flirting with…her. He had been flirting with that pretty blonde.

Faith made sure the door to her office was shut, then she opened up her office drawer, pulling out the mirror she kept in there, that she didn't often use. Just quick checks before meetings. And not to make sure she looked attractive—to make sure she didn't look twelve.

She tilted her chin upward, then to the side, examining her reflection. It was almost absurd to think of him wanting to flirt with her. It wasn't that she was unattractive, it was just that she was…plain.

She had never really cared. Not really.

She could look a little less plain when she threw on some makeup, but then, when she did that, her goal was to look capable and confident, and old enough to be entrusted with the design of someone's house. Not to be pretty.

She twisted her lips to the side, then moved them back, making a kiss face before relaxing again. Then she sighed and put the mirror back in her drawer. It wasn't that she cared. She was a professional. And she wasn't going to…act on any weird feelings she had.

Even if they were plausible.

It was just… When she had talked to Levi last night she had left feeling like a woman. And then she had come into work this morning and her brothers had immediately reset her back to the role of little girl.

She thought about that so effectively that before she knew it, it was time for her to leave to go to Levi's place.

She pulled a bag out of her desk drawer—her makeup bag—and made the snap decision to go for an entirely different look, accomplished with much internet searching for daytime glamour and an easy tutorial. Then she fluffed her hair, shaking it out and making sure the curls looked a little bit tousled.

She threw the bag back into her desk and stood, swaggering out of her office, where she was met by Isaiah, who jerked backward and made a surprised sound.

"What?" she asked.

"You look different."

She waved a hand. "I thought I would try something new."

"You're going to give a talk at one of the… schools?"

"Yes," she said.

"Which school?" he pressed.

She made an exasperated sound. "Why do you need to know?" He said nothing, staring at her with his jaw firmed up. "You need to know because you need it to be in Poppy's planner, because if it's not in Poppy's planner it will feel incomplete to you, is that it?"

She'd long since given up trying to understand her brother's particular quirks. He had them. There was no sense fighting against them. She was his sister, so sometimes she poked at them, rather than doing anything to help him out. That was the way the world worked, after all.

But she'd realized as she'd gotten older that he wasn't being inflexible to be obnoxious. It was something he genuinely couldn't help.

"Yes," he responded, his tone flat.

If he was surprised that she had guessed what the issue was, he didn't show it. But then, Isaiah wouldn't.

"Copper Ridge Elementary," she said, the lie slipping easily past her lips, and she wondered who she was.

A *woman*. That's who she was.

A woman who had made an executive decision about her own career and she did not need her brothers meddling in it.

And her makeup wasn't significant to anything except that she had been sitting there feeling bad about herself and there was no reason to do that when she had perfectly good eyeliner sitting in her desk drawer.

"Thank you," he said.

"Are we done? Can you add it to the calendar and pacify yourself and leave me alone?"

"Is everything okay?" he asked, the question uncharacteristically thoughtful.

"I'm fine, Isaiah. I promise. I'm just… Joshua is right. I've been working a lot. And I don't feel like the solution is to do less. I think it might be…time that I took some initiative, make sure I'm filling my time with things that are important to me."

Of course, she was lying about it being schoolchildren, which made her feel slightly guilty. But not guilty enough to tell the truth.

Isaiah left her office then, to update the planner, Faith assumed. And Faith left shortly after.

She put the address to Levi's house in her car's navigation system and followed the instructions, which led her on much the same route she had taken to get up the mountain to meet him the first time, at the building site. It appeared that his rental property was on the other side of that mountain, on a driveway that led up the opposite side that wound through evergreen trees and took her to a beautiful, rustic-looking structure.

It was an old-fashioned, narrow A-frame with windows that overlooked the valley below. She appreciated it, even if it wasn't something she would ever have put together.

She had a fondness for classic, cozy spaces.

Though her designs always tended toward the open and the modern, she had grown up in a tiny, yellow farmhouse that she loved still. She loved that her parents still lived there in spite of the financial successes of their children.

Of course, Levi's house was several notches above the little farmhouse. This was quite a nice place, even if it was worlds apart from a custom home.

She had been so focused on following the little rabbit trails of thought on her way over that she hadn't noticed the tension she was carrying in her stomach. But as soon as she parked and turned off the engine, she seemed to be entirely made of that tension.

She could hardly breathe around it.

She had seen him outside, out in the open. And she had talked to him in a bar. But she had never been alone indoors with him before.

Not that it mattered. At all.

She clenched her teeth and got out of the car, gathering her bag that contained her sketchbook and all her other supplies. With the beat of each footstep on the gravel drive, she repeated those words in her head.

Not that it mattered.

Not that it mattered.

She might be having some weird thoughts about him, but he certainly wasn't having them about her.

She could only hope that the blonde had vacated before Faith's arrival.

Why did the thought of seeing her here make Faith feel sick? She couldn't answer that question.

She didn't even *know* the guy. And she had never been jealous of anyone or anything in her life. Okay, maybe vague twinges of jealousy that her brothers had found people to love. Or that Hayley had a husband who loved her. That Mia had found someone. And the fact that Mia's someone was Faith's brother made the whole thing a bit inaccessible to her.

But those feelings were more like…envy. This was different. This felt like a nasty little monster on her back that had no right to be there.

She steeled herself, and knocked on the door. And waited.

When the door swung open, it seemed to grab hold of her stomach and pull it along. An intense, sweeping sensation rode through her.

There he was.

Today, he'd traded in the black T-shirt and hat from the last couple of days for white ones.

The whole look was…beautiful and nearly absurd. Because he was *not* a white knight, far from it. And she wasn't innocent enough to think that he was.

But there was something about the way the light color caught hold of those blue eyes and reflected the color even brighter that seemed to steal every thought from her head. Every thought but one.

Beautiful.

She was plain. And this man was *beautiful*.

Oh, not pretty. Scars marred his face and a hard line went through his chin, keeping him from being symmetrical. Another one slashed his top lip. And even then, the angles on his face were far too sharp to be anything so insipid as pretty.

Beautiful.

"Come on in," he said, stepping away from the door.

She didn't know why, but she had expected a little more conversation on the porch. Maybe to give her some time to catch her breath. Sadly, he didn't give it to her. So she found herself following his instructions and walking into the dimly lit entry.

"It's not that great," he said of his surroundings, lifting a shoulder.

"It's cozy," she said.

"Yeah, I'm kind of over cozy. But the view is good."

"I can't say that I blame you," she said, following his lead and making her way into the living area, which was open. The point from the house's A-frame gave height to the ceiling, and the vast windows lit the entire space. The furniture was placed at the center of the room, with a hefty amount of space all around. "That must've been really difficult."

"Are you going to try to absorb details about my taste by asking about my personal life? Because I have to tell you, my aesthetic runs counter to where I've spent the last five years."

"I understand that. And no, it wasn't a leading question. I was just…commenting."

"They started the investigation into my wife's disappearance when you were about eighteen," he said. "And while you were in school I was on house arrest, on trial. Then I spent time behind bars. In that time, you started your business and… Here you are."

"A lot can happen in five years."

"It sure can. Or a hell of a lot of nothing can happen. That's the worst part. Life in a jail cell is monotonous. Things don't change. An exciting day is probably not a good thing. Because it usually means you got stabbed."

"Did you ever get—" her stomach tightened "—stabbed?"

He chuckled, then lifted up his white T-shirt, exposing a broad expanse of tan skin. Her brain processed things in snatches. Another tattoo. A bird, stretched across his side, and then the shifting and bunching of well-defined muscles. Followed by her registering that there was a sprinkling of golden hair across that skin. And then, her eye fell to the raised, ugly scar that was just above the tattooed bird's wing.

"Once," he said.

He pushed his shirt back down, and Faith shifted uncomfortably, trying to settle the feeling that the bird had peeled itself right off his skin and somehow ended up in her stomach, fluttering and struggling for freedom.

She looked away. "What happened?"

She put her hand on her own stomach, trying to calm her response. She didn't know if that intense, unsettled feeling was coming from her horror over what had happened to him, or over the show of skin that had just occurred.

If it was the skin, she was going to be very disappointed in herself and in her hormones. Because the man had just told her he'd been stabbed. Responding to his body was awfully base. Not to mention insensitive.

"I made the motherfucker who did it regret that he'd ever seen me." Suddenly, there was nothing in those ice-blue eyes but cold. And she didn't doubt what he said. Not at all.

"I see."

"You probably don't. And it's for the best. No, I didn't kill him. If I had killed him, I would still be in prison." He sat down in a chair that faced the windows. He rested his arms on the sides, the muscles there flexing as he moved his fingers, clenching them into fists. "But a brawl like that going badly for a couple of inmates? That's easy enough to ignore. I got a few stitches because of a blade. He got a few more because of my fists. People learned quickly not to mess with me."

"Apparently," she said, sitting down on the couch across from him, grateful for the large, oak coffee table between them. "Is any of this furniture yours?"

"No," he responded.

"Good," she replied. "Not that there's anything wrong with it, per se. But—" she knocked on the table "—if you were married to a particular piece it might make it more difficult, design-wise. I prefer to have total freedom."

"I find that in life I prefer to have total freedom," he said, the corner of his mouth quirking upward.

A rash of heat started at Faith's scalp and prickled downward. "Of course. I didn't mean… You know that I didn't…"

"Calm down," he said. "I'm not that easily offended. Unless you stab me."

"Right," she responded. She fished around in her bag until she came up with her notepad. "We should talk more about what you have in mind. Let's start with the specifics. How big do you want the house to be?"

"Big," he replied. "It's a massive lot. The property is about fifty acres, and that cleared-out space seems like there's a lot of scope there."

"Ten thousand square feet?"

"Sure," he responded.

She put her pen over the pad. "How many bedrooms?"

"I should only need one."

"If you don't want more than one, that's okay. But…guests?"

"The only people who are going to be coming to my house are going to be staying in my bed. And even then, not for the whole night."

She cleared her throat. "Right." She tapped her pen against the side of her notebook. "You know, you're probably going to want more bedrooms."

"In case of what? Orgies? Even then, we'd need one big room."

"All right," she said. "If you want an unprecedented one-bedroom, ten-thousand-square-foot house, it's up to you." She fought against the blush flooding her cheeks, because this entire conversation was getting a little earthy for her. And it was making her picture things. Imagining him touching women, and specifically the blonde from last night, and she just didn't need that in her head.

"I wasn't aware I had ordered judgment with my custom home. I thought I ordered an entirely custom home to be done to my specifications."

She popped up her head. Now, this she was used to. Arrogant men who hired her, and then didn't listen.

"You did hire me to design a custom home, but presumably, you wanted my design to influence it. That means I'm going to be giving input. And if I think you're making a decision that's strange or stupid I'm going to tell you. I didn't get where I am by transcribing plans that come from the heads of people who have absolutely no training. If there's one thing I understand, it's buildings. It's design. Homes. I want to take the feeling inside of you and turn it into something concrete. Something real. And I will give you one bedroom if that's what you really want. But if you want a computer program to design your house, then you can have no feedback. I am not a computer program. I'm an...artist."

Okay, that was pushing it a lot further than she usually liked to go. But he was annoying her.

And making her feel hot.

It was unforgivable.

"A mouthy one," he commented.

She sniffed. "I know my value. And I know what I do well."

"I appreciate that quality in...anyone."

"Then appreciate it when I push back. I'm not doing it just for fun."

"If it will make you feel better you can put a few bedrooms in."

"There will definitely be room," she said. "Anyway, think of your resale value."

"Not my concern," he said.

"You never know. You might care about it someday." She cleared her throat. "Now, bathrooms?"

"Put down the appropriate number you think there should be. Obviously, you want me to have multiple bedrooms, I would assume there is an appropriate bathroom number that coincides with that."

"Well, you're going to want a lot. For the orgies." She bit her tongue after she said the words.

"Yeah, true. The last thing you want is for everyone to need a bathroom break at once and for there not to be enough."

She took a deep breath, and let it out slowly. The fact of the matter was, this conversation was serving a bigger purpose. She was forming a lot of ideas about him. Not actually about orgies, but about the fact that he was irreverent. That there was humor lurking inside him, in spite of the darkness. Or maybe in part because of it. That he was tough. Resilient.

That things glanced off him. Like hardship, and knife blades.

A small idea began to form, then expanded into the sorts of things she had been thinking when they had first met. How she could use curves, angles and lines to keep from needing doors, but to also give a sense of privacy, without things feeling closed off.

"Can you stand up?" she asked.

She knew it was kind of an odd question, but she wanted to see where his line of sight fell. Wanted to get an idea of how he would fill the space. He wasn't a family man. His space was going to be all about him. And he had made it very clear that was what he wanted.

She needed to get a sense of him.

"Sure," he responded, pushing himself up onto his feet, arching an eyebrow.

She walked around him, made her way to the window, followed where she thought his line of sight might land. Then she turned to face him, obscuring his view.

"What are you doing?"

"I'm just trying to get a sense for how a room will work for you. For where your eye is going to fall when you look out the window."

"I can send you measurements."

She made a scoffing sound. "You're six foot three."

"I am," he said. "How did you guess?"

"I can visualize measurements pretty damn accurately. I'm always sizing up objects, lots, locations. That's what I do."

"It's still impressive."

"Well, I did have to see you stand before I could fully trust that I was right about your height."

"And how tall are you?"

She stretched up. "Five-two."

A smile curved his lips. "You wouldn't even be able to reach things in my house."

"It's no matter. I can reach things in mine."

"How would you design a house for two people with heights as different as ours?"

She huffed out a laugh, her stomach doing an uncomfortable twist. "Well, obviously when it comes to space, preference has to be given to the taller person so they don't feel like things are closing in on them."

He nodded, his expression mock-serious. "Definitely."

"Mostly, with a family," she said, "which I design for quite a bit, I try to keep things mostly standard in height, with little modifications here and there that feel personal and special and useful to everyone."

"Very nice. Good deflection."

"I wasn't deflecting."

He crossed his arms, his gaze far too assessing. "You seemed uncomfortable."

"I'm not."

"You would want space for a big bed."

"I would?" Her brain blanked. Hollowed out completely.

"If you were designing a room for a man my size. Even if the woman was small."

She swallowed, her throat suddenly dry. "I suppose so."

"But then, I figure there's never a drawback to a big bed."

"I have a referral I can give you for custom furniture," she said, ignoring the way her heart was thundering at the base of her throat, imagining all the things that could be done in a very large bed.

In gauzy terms. Seeing as she had no actual, real-world experience with that.

"I may take you up on that offer," he said, his words like a slow drip of honey.

"Well, good. That's just…great. It's a custom… sex palace." She pretended to write something down, all while trying to hide the fact her face was burning.

"No matter what it sounds like," he said, "I'm not actually asking you for a glorified brothel. Though, I'm not opposed to that being a use. But I want this house to be for me. And I want it to be without limits. I'm tired of being limited."

Her heart twisted. "Right. I—I understand."

She sucked in a sharp breath, and went to move past him, but he spoke again, and his voice made her stop, directly in front of him. "I shared a cell with, at minimum, one other person for the last five years. Everything was standard. Everything. And then sized down. Dirty. Uncomfortable. A punishment. I spent five years being punished for something I didn't do."

She tilted up her face, and realized that she was absurdly close to him. That she was a breath away from his lips. "Now you need your reward."

"That I do."

His voice went low, husky. She felt…unsteady on her feet. Like she wanted to lean in and press her lips to his.

She should move. She was the one who had placed

herself right there in front of him. She was the one who had miscalculated. But she wasn't moving. She was still standing there. She couldn't seem to make herself shift. She licked her lips, and she saw his gaze follow the motion. His eyes were hot again.

And so was she. All over.

She was suddenly overcome by the urge to reach out her hand and touch that scar that marred his chin. The other one that slashed through his lip.

To push her hand beneath his shirt and touch that scar he had shown her earlier.

That thought was enough to bring her back to earth. To bring her back to her senses.

She took a step back, a metallic tang filling her mouth. Humiliation. Fear.

"You know," he said slowly, "they lock men like me up. That's a pretty good indication you should probably keep your distance."

"You didn't do anything," she said.

"That doesn't mean I'm not capable of doing some very bad things." His eyes were hot, so hot they burned. And she should move away from him, but she wasn't.

Heaven help her, she wasn't.

She tried to swallow, but her mouth was so dry her tongue was frozen in place. "Is that a warning? Or a threat?"

"Definitely a warning. For now." He turned away from her and faced the window. "If you listen to it, it'll never have to be a threat."

"Why?"

What she felt right now was a strange kind of emotion. It wasn't anger; it wasn't even fear. It was just a strange kind of resolve. Her brothers already treated her like a child who didn't know her own mind—she wasn't about to let this man do the same thing. Let him issue warnings as if she didn't understand exactly who she was and what she wanted.

She might not know who he was. But she damn well knew who she was.

And she hadn't even done anything. Maybe she wouldn't. Maybe she never would.

But maybe she wanted to, and if she did, the consequences would be on her. It wouldn't be for anyone else to decide.

Least of all this man. This stranger.

"Little girl," he said, his voice dripping with disdain. "If you have to ask why, then you definitely need to take a step back."

Little girl.

No. She wouldn't have this man talk down to her. She had it all over her life, from well-meaning people who loved her. People whose opinions she valued. She wasn't going to let him tell her who she was or what she wanted. To tell her what she could handle.

She didn't step back. She stepped forward.

"I have a feeling you think you're a singular specimen, Levi Tucker. You, with your stab wound and your rough edges." Her heart was thundering, her hands shaking, but she wasn't going to step away. She wasn't going to do what he wanted or expected. "You're not. You're just like every other man I've ever come into contact with. You think you know more than me simply because you're older, or maybe because you have a—a *penis*."

She despised herself for her stutter, but as tough as she was trying to be, she couldn't utter that word a foot away from a man. Not effortlessly. She sucked in a sharp breath. "I'm not exactly sure what gives men such an unearned sense of power. But whatever the reason, you think it's acceptable to talk down to me. Without acknowledging the fact that I have navigated some incredibly difficult waters. They would be difficult for *anyone*, much less someone my age. I'm a lot harder and more filled with resolve than most people will ever be. I don't do warnings or threats. *You* might do well to remember that."

He reached out, the move lightning-fast, and grabbed hold of her wrist. His grip was strong, his hands rough. "And I don't take lectures from prim little misses in pencil skirts. Maybe you'd do well to remember that."

Lightning crackled between them, at the source of his touch, but all around them, too. She was so angry at him. And judging by the fire in his eyes, he was mad at her, too.

She arched forward, and he held her fast, his eyes never leaving hers.

"Do they offer a lot?" she asked. "Prim little misses, I mean. To lecture you?"

"I can't say any of them have ever been able to bring themselves to get this close to me."

She reached out, flexing her fingers, then curled

them into a fist, before resting her fingers flat onto his chest. She could feel his heartbeat raging beneath her hand. She could feel the rhythm echoed in her own labored breathing.

This was insane. She'd never...*ever* touched a man like this before. She'd never wanted to. And she didn't know what kind of crazy had taken over her body, or her mind, right then.

She only knew that she wanted to keep touching him. That she liked the way it felt to have him holding tightly to her wrist.

That she relished the feeling of his heartbeat against her skin.

He smelled good. Like the pine trees and the mountain air, and she wondered if he'd been outside before she'd come over.

A man who couldn't be contained by walls. Not now.

And her literal job was to create a beautiful new cage for him.

She suddenly felt the urge to strip him of everything. All his confines. All his clothes. To make him free.

To be free with him.

The urge was strong—so strong—she was almost shocked to find she hadn't begun to pull at his T-shirt.

But what would she even do if she...succeeded?

He released his hold then, but she could still feel his touch lingering long after he'd taken away his hand. She felt dazed, thrown.

Stunned to discover the world hadn't collapsed

around them in those moments that had seemed like hours, but had actually been a breath.

"You should go."

She should. She really, really should.

But she didn't want him to know he'd scared her. *It's not even him that scares you. You're scaring yourself.*

"I'm going to go sketch," she said, swallowing hard. "This has been very enlightening."

"If your plan is to go off and design me a prison cell now…"

"No," she said. "I'm a professional. But trust me, I've learned quite a bit about you. And my first question to you wasn't leading, not necessarily. But everything that we've discussed here? It will definitely end up being fodder for the design. You're truly going to be in a prison of your own making by the time I'm through, Levi. So you best be sure you like what you're using to build it."

She didn't know where she got the strength, or the wit, for all of that. And by the time she turned on her heel and walked out of the A-frame, heading back to her car, she was breathing so hard she thought she might collapse.

But she didn't.

No, instead she got in her car and drove away, that same rock-solid sense of resolve settling in her stomach now that had been there only a moment before.

Attraction.

Was that what had just happened back there? Attraction to a man who seemed hell-bent on warning her off.

Why would he want to warn her off?

If he really did see her as a little girl, if he really did see her as someone uninteresting or plain, he wouldn't need to warn her away.

What he'd said about threats...

By the time she pulled back into GrayBear Construction, she wasn't hyperventilating anymore, but she was certain of one thing.

Levi Tucker was attracted to her, too.

She was not certain exactly what she was supposed to do with that knowledge.

She felt vaguely helpless knowing she couldn't ask anyone, either.

Her brothers would go on a warpath. Hayley would caution her. Mia would... Well, Mia would tell Devlin, because Devlin was her husband and she wouldn't want to keep secrets from him.

Faith's network was severely compromised. For one moment that made her feel helpless. Then in the next...

It was her decision, she realized.

Whatever she did with this... It was her decision.

She wasn't a child. And she wasn't going to count on the network of people she was used to having around her to make the choice for her.

And she wasn't going to worry about what they might think.

Whatever she decided...

It would be her choice.

And whatever happened as a result… She would deal with the consequences.

The resolve inside of her only strengthened.

Six

He was back at the bar. Because there was nothing else to do. As of today, he was officially a divorced man, and he'd been without sex for five years.

And earlier today he had been about a breath away from taking little Miss Prim and Proper down to the ground and fucking her senseless.

And he had already resolved that he wouldn't do that. He wouldn't *be* that.

His postdivorce celebration would not be with Faith Grayson. With her wide eyes and easy blush. And uncommon boldness.

He couldn't work out why she wasn't afraid of him. He had thought... A little, soft thing like her... The evidence of a knife fight and talk of prison, jokes about orgies... It all should have had a cowering effect on her.

It hadn't.

No, by the end of the interaction she'd only grown bolder. And he couldn't for the life of him figure out how that worked.

She was fascinated by him. That much was clear. She might even think she wanted to have a little fun with some kind of bad-boy fantasy, but the little fool had no idea.

He was nobody's fantasy.

He was a potential nightmare, but that was it.

He flashed back to the way it had felt to wrap his hand around her wrist. Her skin soft beneath his. To the way she'd looked up at him, her breath growing choppy and fast.

Those fingertips on his chest.

Shit, he needed to get laid.

He ordered up a shot of whiskey and pounded it down hard, scanning the room, looking for a woman who might wipe the image of Faith Grayson from his mind.

Maybe Mindy would be back. Maybe they could pick up where they left off.

But as he looked around, his eye landed on a petite brunette standing in line for the mechanical bull. She was wearing a tight pair of blue jeans and a fitted T-shirt, and when she turned, he felt like he'd been punched in the stomach.

Faith Grayson.

With that same mulish expression on her face she'd had when she'd left his house earlier.

The rider in front of her got thrown, and Faith

rubbed her hands together, glaring at the mechanical beast with intensity. Then she marched up to it and took her position.

She thrust her hips forward, wrapping one hand around the handle and holding the other up high over her head. She looked more like a ballerina than a bull rider. But her expression…

That was all fire.

He should look away. He sure as hell shouldn't watch as the mechanical bull began its forward motion, shouldn't watch the way Faith's eyes widened, and then the way her face turned determined as she gripped more tightly with one hand, and tensed her thighs around the beast, moving her hips in rhythm with it.

It didn't last long.

On the creature's second roll forward, Faith was unseated, her lips parting in an expression of shock as she flew forward and onto the mats below.

And before he could stop himself, he was on his feet, making his way across the space. She was on her back, her chin-length curls spread around her head like a halo on a church window. But her expression was anything but angelic.

"Are you okay?" he asked.

She looked up at him, and all the shock drained from her face, replaced instead by a spark of feral-looking rage. "What are you doing here?"

"What are you doing getting on the back of that thing?" He moved closer, ignoring the crowd of people looking on. "You clearly have no business doing it."

"It's not your business…what I have business doing or not doing. Stop trying to tell me what to do."

He put out his hand, offering to take hold of hers and help her up, but she ignored him, pushing herself into a sitting position and scrabbling to her feet.

"I'm fine," she said.

"I know you're fine," he returned. "It's not like I thought the thing was going to jump off its post and trample you to death. But it's also clear you're being an idiot."

"Well, look at the whole line of idiots," she said, indicating the queue of people. "I figured I would join in."

"Why, exactly?"

"Because," she said. "Because I'm tired of everyone treating me like a kid. Because I'm tired of everyone telling me what to do. Do you know that it was almost impossible for me to sneak away to our meeting today because my brothers need to know what I'm doing every second of every day? It's like they think I'm still fifteen years old."

He shrugged. "As I understand it, that's older brothers, to a degree."

"Are you an older brother?"

"No," he said. "Only child. But still, seems a pretty logical conclusion."

"Well, whatever. I went to boarding school from the time I was really young. Because there were more opportunities for me there than here. I lived away from my family, and somehow…everyone is more protective of me. Like I didn't have to go make my own way when I was a kid." She shook her head. "I mean, granted, it was an all-girls boarding school, and it was a pretty cloistered environment. But still."

"Let me buy you a drink," he said, not quite sure why the offer slipped out.

You know.

He ignored that.

"I don't need you to buy me a drink," she said fiercely, storming past him and making her way to the bar. "I can buy my own drink."

"I'm sure you can. But I offered to do it. You should let me."

"Yeah, you have a lot of opinions about what I should and shouldn't do in a given moment, don't you?"

Still, when he ordered her a rum and Coke, she didn't argue. She took hold of it and leaned against the bar, angling toward him. His eyes dropped down to her breasts, a hard kick of lust making it difficult for him to breathe.

"What are you doing here?" He forced his gaze away from her breasts, to her face.

She narrowed her eyes. "I'm here to ride a mechanical bull and make a statement about my agency by doing so. Not to anyone but myself, mind you. It might be silly, but it is my goal. What's yours?"

"I'm here to get laid," he said, holding her eyes and not blinking. That should do the trick. That should scare her away.

Unless…

She tilted her head to the side. "Is that what you were here for last night?"

"Yes, ma'am," he responded.

Her lips twitched, and she lifted up her glass, averting her gaze. "How was she?" She took a sip of the rum and Coke.

"As it happens," he said, "I didn't go home with her."

She spluttered, then set down the glass on the bar and looked at him. She didn't bother to disguise her interest. Her curiosity. "Why?"

"Because I decided at the end of it all I wasn't really that interested. No one was more surprised by that than I was."

"She was beautiful," Faith said. "Why weren't you…into her?"

He firmed his jaw, looking Faith up and down. "That is the million-dollar question, honey."

That same thing that had stretched between them back at the house began to build again. It was like a physical force, and no matter that he told himself she was all wrong, his body seemed to disagree.

You dumbass. You want something harder than she can give. Something dirtier. You don't want to worry about your partner. You want a partner who can handle herself.

But then he looked back at Faith again, her cheeks rosy from alcohol and the exertion of riding the bull, and maybe from him.

He wanted her.

And there wasn't a damn thing he could do to change that.

"I have a theory," Faith said.

"About?"

"About why you didn't want her." She sucked her straw between her lips and took a long sip, then looked up at him, as if fortified by her liquid courage. "Is it because...?" She tilted her chin upward, her expression defiant. "Are you attracted to me, Levi?"

He gritted his teeth, the blood in his body rushing south, answering the question as soon as she asked it. "You couldn't handle me, baby girl."

"That's not what I asked you."

"But it's an important thing for you to know."

She shrugged her shoulders. "That's what you think. Again, putting you on the long list of men who think they know what I should and shouldn't do, or want, or think about."

He leaned in and watched as the color in her cheeks deepened. As that crushed-rose color bloomed more fully. She was playing the part of seductress—at least, in her funny little way—but she wasn't as confident as she was hoping to appear. That much he could tell.

"Do you have any idea what I would do to you?" he asked.

She wrinkled her nose. "I would assume...the normal sort of thing."

He chuckled. "Sweetheart, I was locked up for five years. I'm not sure I remember what the normal sort of thing is anymore. At this point, all I have to go on is animal instinct. And I'm not totally sure you should feel comfortable with that."

She shifted, and he noticed her squeezing her thighs together. The sight sent a current of lust straight through his body. Dammit. He was beginning to think he had underestimated her.

"That still isn't what I asked you," she said softly. She looked up at him, her expression coy as she gazed through her thick lashes. "Do you want me?"

"I'd take you," he said through gritted teeth. "Hard. And believe me, you'd like it. But I don't want *you*, sweetheart. I just want. It's been a hell of a long time for me, Faith. I'm all about the sex, not the woman. I'm not sure that's the kind of man you should be with."

She squared her shoulders and looked at him full on, but the color in her cheeks didn't dissipate. "What kind of man do you think I should be with?"

He could see it. Like a flash of lightning across the darkness in his soul. A man who would get down on one knee and ask Faith to be his. Have babies with her. Live with her, in a house with a lot of bedrooms for all those babies.

A man she could take to family dinners. Hold hands with.

A man who could care.

That was what she deserved.

"One who will be nice to you," he said, moving closer. "One you can take home to your family." He cupped her cheek, swept his thumb over her lower lip and felt her tremble beneath his touch. "A man who will make love to you." She tilted her face upward, pressing that tempting mouth more firmly against his thumb. "All I can do is fuck you, sweetheart."

She looked down, then back up. And for once, she didn't have a comeback.

"You deserve a man who will marry you," he continued.

That mobilized her. "Get married? And then what? Have children? I'm twenty-five years old and my career is just starting to take off. Why would I do anything to interrupt that? Why would you think that's what I'm looking for right now? I have at least ten years before worrying about any of that. A few affairs in the meantime…"

He snorted. "Affairs. That sounds a hell of a lot more sophisticated and fancy than what I've got in mind, princess."

"What have I ever done to make you think I'm a princess? To make you think I need you to offer more than what I'm standing here showing interest in? You don't have access to my secret heart, Levi."

"If you had any sense in your head, you would walk out of this bar and forget we had this conversation. Hell, if you had any sense at all you would forget today happened. Just do the job I hired you to do and walk away. My wife let me go to jail for her murder while she was alive. And whatever the authorities think, whatever she says…"

He bit down hard, grinding his teeth together. "She was going to let me rot there, in a jail cell. While letting me think she was dead. Do you know…

I grieved her, Faith. I didn't know she was in hiding. I didn't know she had left me on her own feet. All I knew was that she was gone, and that I hadn't killed her. But I believed some other bastard had. My motivation while I was in prison was to avenge my wife, and in the end? She's the one who did this to me." He laughed hard, the sound void of humor. "Love is a lie. Marriage is a joke. And I'm not going to change my mind about that."

"Marriage is an impediment to what I want," Faith said. "And I'm not going to change my mind about that. You're acting like you know what I want. What I should want. But you don't."

"What do you want, sweetheart? Because all I've got to give you is a few good orgasms."

She drew in a sharp breath, blinking a couple of times. Then she looked around the bar, braced herself on the counter and drew up on her toes as high as she could go, pressing a kiss to the lower corner of his mouth. When she pulled away, her eyes were defiant.

If she was playing chicken with him, if she was trying to prove something, she was going to regret it. Because he was not a man who could be played with.

Not without consequences.

He wrapped his arm around her waist, crossed her to his chest and hauled her up an extra two inches so their mouths could meet more firmly.

And that's when he realized he had made a mistake.

He had been of a mind that he would scare her

off, but what he hadn't anticipated was the way his own control would be so tenuous.

He had none. None at all.

Because he hadn't been this close to a woman in more than five years. And he'd imagined his wife a victim. Kidnapped or killed. And when he'd thought of her his stomach had turned. And not knowing what had happened to Alicia…

It hadn't felt right to think of anyone else.

So for most of those five years in prison he hadn't even had a good go-to fantasy. It had been so long since he'd been with a woman who hadn't betrayed him, and it was hard for him to remember a woman other than his wife.

But now… Now there was Faith.

And she burned brighter, hotter, than the anger in his veins. He forgot why he had been avoiding this. Forgot everything but the way she tasted.

It was crazy.

Of all the women he could touch, he shouldn't touch her. She worked for him. He had hired her to design his house and he supposed that made this the worst idea of all.

But she was kissing him back as though it didn't matter.

Maybe he was wrong about her. Maybe she made a habit of toying with her rich and powerful clients. Maybe that was part of why she'd gotten to where she was.

No skin off his nose if it was true. And it suited

him in many ways, because that meant she knew the rules of the game.

Because you need justification for the fact that you're doing exactly what you swore to yourself you wouldn't?

Maybe his reaction had nothing to do with his ex-wife making him into a monster. Maybe it had everything to do with Faith making him a beast.

Uncontrolled and ravenous for everything he could get.

He cupped her chin, forcing her lips apart, and thrust his tongue deep. And she responded. She responded beautifully. Hot and slick and enthusiastic.

"You better give an answer and stick to it," he said when they pulled away, his eyes intent on hers. "Say yes or no now. Because once we leave this bar—"

"Yes," she said quickly, a strange, frantic energy radiating from her. "Yes. Let's do it."

"This isn't a business deal, honey."

"That's why I didn't shake your hand." She sounded breathless, and a little bit dazed, and dammit all if it wasn't a thousand times more intoxicating than Mindy's careful seduction from last night.

"Then let's go." Now he was in a damn hurry. To get out of here before she changed her mind. Before he lost control completely and took her against a wall.

"What about my car?" she asked.

"I'll get you back to it."

"Okay," she said.

He put down a twenty on the bar, and ignored the

way the bartender stared at him, hard and unfriendly-like, as though the man had an opinion about what was going on.

"Tell the man you're with me," he said.

Faith's eyes widened, and then she looked between him and the bartender. "I'm with him," she said softly.

The bartender's expression relaxed a fraction. But only a fraction.

Then Levi took her hand and led her out into the night. The security lights in the lot were harsh, bright blue, and she still looked beautiful beneath them. That was as close to poetry as he was going to get. Because everything else was all fire. Fire and need, and the sense that if he didn't get inside her in the next few minutes, he was going to explode.

"Levi..."

He grabbed her and pulled her to him, kissing her again, dark and fierce and hard. "Last chance," he said, because he wasn't a gentleman, but he wasn't a monster, either.

"Yes."

Seven

Faith felt giddy. Drunk on her own bravery. Her head was swimming, arousal firing through her veins. She had never felt like this before. Ever. She had gone on a couple of dates, all of which had ended with sad, sloppy kisses at the door and no desire at all on her part for it to go any further.

She had begun to think the only thing she was really interested in was her career. That men were irrelevant, and if men were, then sex was, too. She had just figured that was how she was. That maybe, when the time came, and she was ready to settle down, or ready to pull back on her career, she would find her priorities would naturally restructure and sex would suddenly factor in. But she hadn't worried about it.

And now... It wasn't a matter of making herself

interested. No. It was a matter of life and death. At least it felt like it might be.

He took her hand to his heart, and helped her into his truck. She didn't say a word as he started the engine and they pulled out of the parking lot.

Her heart was thundering, and she was seriously questioning her sanity. To go from her first makeout session to sex in only a few minutes might not be the best idea, but it might also be…the only way. She was half out of her mind with desire, just from feeling his lips on hers. Even so, she honestly couldn't imagine wanting more than sex.

This man, her secret.

It had been almost funny when he had said something about taking a man home to meet her family. There would be no way she could ever take him home to meet her parents.

His frame would be so large and ridiculous in that tiny farmhouse. The ice in his veins, the scars on his soul, so much more pronounced in that warm, sweet kitchen of her mother's.

No, Faith didn't want to take him home. She wanted him to take her to bed.

And maybe it was crazy. But she had never intended to save herself for anything in particular. Anything but desire, really.

And this was the first time she had ever felt it.

What better way to get introduced to sex, really? An older man who knew exactly what he was doing. Because God knew she didn't.

And for once, she wasn't going to think. She wasn't going to worry about the future, wasn't going to worry about anyone else's opinion, because no one was ever going to know.

Levi Tucker was already her dirty secret in her professional life. Why couldn't he be her personal one, too?

Suddenly, he jerked the car off the highway, taking it down a narrow, dirt road and into the woods. "This isn't the way to your house."

"Can't wait," he growled.

"What's this?" she asked, her heart pounding in her chest.

"A place I know about from way back. Back when I used to get in trouble around these parts."

Get in trouble.

That's what she was about to do. Get in trouble with him.

She felt…absolutely elated. She had gone out to the bar tonight to do *something*. To shake things up. She had seen riding the bull as a kind of kickoff tour for her mini Independence Day.

Oh, it wasn't one she was going to flaunt in front of her brothers or anything like that. It was just acknowledging that sense of resolve from earlier. She was going to have something that was just hers. Choices that were hers.

It had all started with taking this job, she realized. So, it was fitting that the rest of it would involve Levi, too.

"Okay," she said.

"Still good?"

She gritted her teeth, and then made a decision, feeling much bolder than she should have. She moved her hand over and pressed it against his thigh. He was hard, hot. Then she slid her hand farther up, between his legs, capturing his length through denim. He was big. Oh, Lord, he was big. She hadn't realized… Well, that just went to show how ignorant she was. Maybe he was average, she didn't know. But it was a hell of a lot bigger than she had imagined it might be.

It was going to be inside her.

Her internal muscles clenched, and she realized that rather than fear, she was overcome completely by excitement. Maybe that was the perk of waiting twenty-five years to lose your virginity. She was past ready.

He growled, jerking his car off the road and to a turnout spot next to the trees. Then he unbuckled his seat belt and moved over to the center of the bench seat, undoing her belt and hauling her into his lap. He kissed her, deep and hard, matching what had happened back at the bar.

Her head was spinning, her whole body on fire.

He stripped off her T-shirt, quickly and ruthlessly, his fingers deft on her bra. She didn't even have time to worry about it. Didn't have time to think. Her breasts were bare, and he was cupping them, sliding calloused thumbs over her nipples, teasing her, enticing her.

She felt like she was flying.

She wanted him to take her wherever this was going. She wanted him to take control. She was used to being the one in control. The one who knew what she was doing. She was a natural in her field, and that meant she always walked in knowing what she was doing. Being the novice was a strange, amazing feeling, and she had the sense that if she'd been with a man any less masterful, it might feel diminishing.

Instead it just felt like—like a weight on her shoulders suddenly lifted. Because he was bearing responsibility for all these feelings of pleasure in her body. He was stoking the need, and soothing it just as quickly. But all the while, a deep, endless ache was building between her legs and she wanted… She needed… She didn't know.

But she knew that he knew. Oh, yes, he did.

He kissed her neck, cupping her head as he moved lower, as he captured one nipple between his lips and sucked her in deep. It was so erotic, so filthy, and she couldn't do anything but arch into his touch as he moved his attention to her other breast. He was fulfilling fantasies she hadn't even known she'd had.

She had just never…thought about doing such a thing. And here he was, not only making it seem appealing, but it was also as if she might die if she didn't have it.

He pulled his own shirt over his head, tugging her heart against his chest, his muscles, the hair there, adding delicious friction against her nipples, and she squirmed. He wrapped his arm tightly around her waist, cupped her head and laid her back, somehow managing to strip her of her jeans and panties in re-cord time in the close confines of the truck. Then he took hold of the buckle on his belt, and she heard the rasp of fabric and metal as he worked the leather strap through, as he undid the zipper on his jeans.

She jumped when he pressed his hand between her thighs, moved his fingers through her slickness, drawing the moisture up over that sensitized bun-dle of nerves, then slid his thumb expertly back and forth, creating a kind of tension inside her she wasn't sure she could withstand.

"I'll make it last longer later," he said gruffly. "Promise."

But she didn't really understand what he meant, and when she heard the tearing of a plastic packet, she only dimly registered what was about to hap-pen. Then he was kissing her again, and she didn't think. Until the blunt head of his arousal was push-ing into her body, until he thrust hard and deep, a fierce, burning sensation claiming any of the plea-sure she had felt a moment before.

She cried out, digging her fingernails into his shoulders, trying to blot out the pain that was roll-ing through her like a storm.

"Faith…"

She tensed up, turning her head away, freezing for a moment. "Don't say anything," she whispered.

"Sorry," he said, sinking more deeply into her, a groan on his lips. "You feel so damn good."

And that tortured admission did something to her, ignited something deep inside her that went past pain. That went past fear. The scary part was over. It was done. And the pain was already beginning to roll itself back.

"Don't stop," she whispered, curling her fingers around his neck and holding on as she shifted beneath him.

It was strange, this feeling. His body inside hers. How had she not realized? How intimate something like this would be?

Everybody talked about sex at university. Gave great proclamations about what they liked and what they didn't, had endless discussions about the *when*, the *why* and the *with who*. But no one had ever said sex made you feel like someone hadn't just entered your body, but your whole soul. No one had said that you would want to run away and draw closer at the same time.

No one had said that it would be a great, wrenching pain followed by a deep, strange sense of connection that seemed to bloom into desire again as he shifted his hips and arched into her.

She tested what it might feel like if she moved against him, too, and found that she liked it. With each and every thrust that he made into her body, animalistic sounds coming from deep inside of him, she met him. Until her body was slick with sweat— his or hers, she didn't know. Until that fierce need she had felt the first time he had kissed her was back. Until she thought she might die if she didn't get more of him.

Until she no longer wanted to run at all.

He growled, his hardness pulsing inside her as he froze above her, slamming back into her one last time. And then, a release broke inside her like a wave, and she found herself drowning. In pleasure. In him.

And when he looked at her, she suddenly felt small and fragile. Any sense of being resolute crumbled.

And much to her horror, a tear slid down her cheek.

She was crying. God in heaven, the woman was crying.

No. He wasn't going to think about God. Not right now. Because God had nothing to do with this. No, this was straight from hell, and he was one of the devil's chosen. There was no other way to look at it.

Not only had he taken her in his truck like a beast—a fancy justification for sidestepping the word *monster* if ever there was one—but she had also been a virgin.

And he hadn't stopped.

When he had hit that resistance, when he had seen that flash of pain on her face, he had waited only a moment before he kept on going. She'd lifted her hips, and he hadn't been able to do anything but keep going. Because she was beautiful. And he wanted her. More than beautiful, she was soft and delicate, and an indulgence.

And he hadn't had any of that for more than five years.

Sinking into her tight body had been a revelation. As much as a damnation.

"Dammit to hell," he muttered, straightening and pulling his pants back into place. He chucked the condom out the window, not really giving a damn what happened to it later.

"What?" she asked, her petite frame shivering, shaking, her arms wrapped tightly around her body, as though she was trying to protect herself.

Too little, too late.

"You know."

"I don't," she said, shrinking more deeply into the far corner of the truck, her pale figure cast into a soft glow by the moonlight. "I don't... I thought it was good."

Her voice was trembling, watery, and he could hear the sigh that she breathed out becoming a sob.

"You didn't tell me you were a virgin," he said, trying to keep the accusation out of his voice, because dammit, he had known. On some level, he had known. And he hadn't been put off by it at all.

No, he had *told* himself to be put off by it. By her obvious innocence and inexperience. He had commanded himself not to be interested in it. To chase after someone more like him. Someone a little bit dark. Someone a little bit craven. But his body didn't want that.

Because his soul was a destroyer. A consumer of everything good and sweet.

Hadn't Alicia been sweet when he'd met her? Hadn't she transformed into something else entirely over their time together? How could he ignore the fact that he was the common denominator at the center of so many twisted scenarios in his life?

Him.

The one thing he could never fully remove from the equation unless he removed himself from the world.

"So what?" she asked, shuffling around in the car, undoubtedly looking for her clothes. "I knew that."

"I damn well didn't."

"What does it have to do with anything?"

"You told me you knew what you were doing."

"I did," she said, her voice shrinking even smaller. "I knew exactly what we were going to do." She made a soft, breathy laugh. "I mean, I didn't know that we were going to do it in the truck. I expected it to take a little bit…longer. But I knew we were going to have sex."

"You're crying."

"That's my problem," she said.

"No," he said, reaching across the space and dragging her toward him. He gripped her chin between his thumb and forefinger and gazed into her eyes. It was dark, but he could see the glitter in her gaze. Like the stars had fallen down from the sky and centered themselves in her. "Now it's my problem."

"It doesn't have to be. I made a choice. My lack of experience doesn't make it less my choice."

"Yes, it does. Because you didn't really know. I hurt you. And because you didn't tell me, I hurt you worse than I would have."

"Again, that's on me. I wanted to have sex with

an older guy. One who knew what he was doing. I'm way too old to be a virgin, Levi. I never found someone I wanted to change that with, and then I met you and I wanted you. It seems simple to me."

"Simple."

The top of his head had just about blown off. Nothing about this seemed simple to him.

"Yes," she said.

"Little girl, I hadn't had sex in more than five years. You don't want a man like me in bed with you. You want a nice man who has the patience to take time with your body."

"But I like *your* body. And I like the way it made mine feel."

"I hurt you," he pointed out.

She lifted a pale shoulder. "It felt good at the end."

"Doesn't matter. That's all I have. Rough and selfish. That's what I am. It's all I want to be."

"Well, I want to be my own person. I want to be someone who makes her own choices and doesn't give a damn what anyone else thinks. So maybe we're about perfect for each other right now."

"Right now."

"Yes," she said. "I don't know why you find it so hard to believe, but I really do know what I want. Do you think I'm going to fall in love with you, Levi?"

She spoke the words with such disdainful incredulity, and if he was a different man, with a softer heart—with a heart at all—he might've been offended. As it was, he found her open scorn almost amusing.

"Virgins fall in love with all kinds of assholes, sweetheart."

"Have you deflowered a lot of them?"

"No. I haven't been with a damn virgin since I was one."

"Then maybe calm down with your pronouncements." She was wiggling back into her jeans now, then pulling her top over her head. She hadn't bothered to put her bra back on. And he was the perverse bastard who took an interest in that.

"I'm a lot more experienced than you. Maybe you should recognize that my pronouncements come from a place of education."

"It's done," she said. "And you know what? It was fine. It was fine until this."

"I'll take you home."

"Take me back to my car," she said.

"I'd rather not drop you back in the parking lot at this hour."

"Take me back to my damn car," she said. "I don't want to arrange a ride later. I don't need my car sitting in the parking lot all night, where people can draw conclusions."

"You didn't mind that earlier."

"Well, earlier I didn't feel bad or ashamed about my choices, but you've gone and made that… It's different now. It's different."

If he had a conscience, he would have felt guilt over that. But it wasn't guilt that wracked his body now. It was rage.

Rage that the monster had won.

The rage had nothing to do with her. Nothing about the way it might impact her life. It was about him.

Maybe that was selfish. He didn't really know. Didn't really care, either.

"If you'd like to withdraw from the job, I understand," he said when they pulled back into the parking lot of Ace's bar.

"Hell, no," she said, her tone defiant. "I'm not losing this job. You don't get to ruin that, too."

"I wouldn't figure you'd want to work with me anymore."

"You think you know a lot about me. For a man who knows basically nothing. The whole…intimacy-of-sex thing is a farce. You have no idea who I am. You have no idea what I want, what I need. I will finish this job because I took it on. And when I said that I wanted you, when I said I wanted this, I knew we were going to continue working together."

"Suit yourself."

"None of this suits me."

She tumbled out of the truck and went to her car, and he waited until she was inside, until she got it started and began to pull out of the space, before he started heading back toward his place.

But it wasn't until he parked in front of his house that he realized she had left her bra and panties behind.

The two scraps of fabric seemed to represent the final shreds of his humanity.

He reached out and touched her bra, ran his thumb over the lace.

And he asked himself why the hell he was bothering to pull away now. She had been…a revelation. Soft and perfect and everything he'd ever wanted.

He wondered why the hell he was pretending he cared about being a man, when being a monster was so much easier.

Eight

One thought kept rolling through Faith's mind as she sat at her desk and tried to attend to her work.

She wasn't a virgin anymore.

She had lost her virginity. In a pickup truck.

Of all the unexpected turns of events that had occurred in her life, this was inarguably the *most* unexpected. She surely had not thought she would do that, ever.

Not the virginity thing. She had been rather sanguine about that. She had known sex would happen eventually, and there was no point in worrying about it.

But the pickup truck. She had really not seen herself as a do-it-in-a-pickup-truck kind of girl.

With a man like that.

If she actually sat and broke down her thoughts on what kind of man she had imagined she might be with, it wasn't him. Not even a little bit. Not even at all.

She had imagined she would find a man quite a bit like herself. Someone who was young, maybe. And understood what it was like to be ambitious at an early age. Someone who could relate to her. Her particular struggles.

But then, she supposed, that was more relationship stuff. And sex didn't require that two people be similar. Only that they ignited when they touched.

She certainly hadn't imagined it would be an ex-convict accused of murder who would light her on fire.

Make her come.

Make her cry.

Then send her away.

It had been a strange twelve hours indeed.

"Faith?" She looked up and saw Isaiah standing in the doorway. "I need estimates from you."

"Which estimates?" She blinked.

"The ones you haven't sent me yet," he said, being maddeningly opaque and a pain in the ass. He could just tell her.

She cleared her throat, tapping her fingers together. Hoping to buy herself some time. Or a clue. "Is there a particular set of estimates that you're waiting on?"

"If you have any estimates put together that I don't have, I would like them."

She realized that she didn't have any for him. And if she should…

That meant she had dropped the ball.

She never dropped the ball.

She had been working, full tilt, at this job for enough years now that she had anticipated the moment when she might drop the ball, but she hadn't. And now she had taken on this extra project, this work her brothers didn't know about, and she was messing up.

That isn't why…

No, it wasn't.

She was messing up because she felt consumed. Utterly and completely consumed by everything that was happening with Levi.

Levi Tucker was so much more than just an interesting architecture project.

It was the structure of the man himself that had her so invested. Not what she might build for him.

She wanted to see him again. Wanted to talk to him. Wanted to lie down in a bed with him, with the lights on so she could look at all his tattoos and trace the lines of them.

So she could know him.

Right. That makes sense. He's nothing like you thought you wanted. Why are you fixating?

A good question.

She didn't want him to be right. Right about virgins and how they fell in love as easy as some people stumbled while walking down the street.

"Faith?"

Isaiah looked concerned now.

"I'm fine," she said.

"You don't look fine."

"I am." She shifted, feeling a particular soreness between her legs and trying to hide the blush that bled into her cheeks. It was weird to be conscious of that while she was talking to her brother.

"Faith, no one has ever accused me of being particularly perceptive when it comes to people's emotions. But I do know you. I know that you're never late with project work. If all of this has become too much for you…"

"It isn't," she insisted. "I love what we do. I'm so proud of what we've built, Isaiah. I'm not ever going to do anything to compromise that. I think I might have overextended myself a little bit with… extra stuff."

"What kind of extra stuff?"

"Just…community work."

Getting screwed senseless for the first time in my life…

"You don't need to do that. Joshua can handle all of that. It's part of his job. You should filter it all through him. He'll help you figure out what you should say yes to, what you can just send a signed letter to…"

"I know. I know you'll both help me. But at some point… Isaiah, this is *my* life." She took a breath. "We are partners. And I appreciate all that you do. If I had to calculate the finances like you, I would go insane. My brain would literally leak out of my ears."

"It would not literally leak out of your ears."

She squinted. "You don't know that."

"I'm pretty confident that I do."

She shook her head. "Just don't worry about me. You have a life now. A really good one. I'm so happy for you and Poppy. I'm so excited for your baby, and for...everything. You've spent too many years working like a crazy person."

"Like a robot," Isaiah said, lifting his brow. "At least, that's what I've been told more than once."

"You're not a robot. You came here to check on me. That makes it obvious that you aren't. But, you also can't carry everything for me. Not anymore. It's just not... I don't need you to. It's okay."

"You know we worry. We worry because you're right. If it weren't for us...then you wouldn't be in this position."

She made a scoffing sound. "Thanks. But if it weren't for me you wouldn't be in this position, either."

"I know," he returned. "I mean, I would still be working in finance somewhere else. Joshua would be doing PR. And you would no doubt be working at a big firm somewhere. But it's what we could do together that has brought our business to this level. And I think Joshua and I worry sometimes that it happened really quickly for you and we enabled that. So, we don't want to leave it all resting on your shoulders now."

She swallowed hard. "I appreciate that. I do. But I can handle it."

Isaiah nodded slowly and then turned and walked out of her office.

She could handle all of this.

Her job, which encouraged her to open up some files for her various projects and collect those estimates Isaiah was asking for, and this new turn of events with Levi.

She was determined to finish the project. The idea of leaving it undone didn't work for her. Not at all. Even if he was being terrible.

And you think you can be in the same room with him and not feel like you're dying?

She didn't know. She had just lost her virginity twelve hours ago, and she had no idea what she was supposed to do next.

Sitting at her desk and basking in that achievement was about all she could do. It was lunchtime when she got into her car and began to drive.

She had spent the rest of the morning trying to catch up, and as soon as she got on the road her thoughts began to wander. Back to what Levi had said to her last night. All the various warnings he had given. About how rough he was. How broken. And in truth, he had not been gentle. But none of it had harmed her. It might have hurt her momentarily, but that pain wasn't something she minded.

Maybe...

Maybe he had been right.

Maybe the whole thing was something she'd been ill-prepared for. Something she shouldn't have pushed for. Because, while physically she had been completely all right with everything that had happened, emotionally she wasn't okay with being pushed away.

And maybe that was the real caution in this story.

He had gone on and on about all that he believed she could handle and she had imagined he meant what she could handle from a sexual-sophistication standpoint. Moves and skills and the knowledge of how things went between men and women.

But that had been the easy part. Following his lead. Allowing his hands, his mouth, his… All of him, to take her on a journey.

But afterward…

She frowned, and it was only then that she realized which direction she was driving.

And she knew she had a choice.

She could keep on going, or she could turn back.

But even as she thought it, she knew the truth. It was too late.

She couldn't go back.

She might have a better understanding of things after last night, and with everything she knew now, she might have made a different decision in that bar.

But she had to go forward.

With that in mind, she turned onto the winding road that led up to Levi's house.

And she didn't look back.

When Levi heard the knock on his door, he was less than amused. He was not in the mood to be preached at, subjected to a sales pitch or offered Girl

Scout cookies. And he could legitimately think of no other reason why anyone would be knocking on his door. So he pulled it open on a growl, and then froze.

"You're not a Jehovah's Witness."

Faith cleared her throat. "Not last I checked." She lifted a shoulder. "I'm Baptist, but—"

"That's not really relevant."

Her lips twitched. "Well… I guess not to *this* conversation, no."

"What are you doing here?"

"I felt like I was owed a chance to have a conversation with you when I wasn't naked and waiting to be returned to my car."

When she put it like that… He felt like even more of a dick. He hadn't thought that was possible.

"Go ahead," he said, extending his hand out.

"Oh. I didn't think… Maybe you should invite me in?"

"Should I?"

"It would be the polite thing to do."

"Well, you'll have to forgive me. In all the excitement of the last few years of my life, I've forgotten what the polite thing is."

"Oh, that's BS." And she breezed past him and stamped into the house. "I understand that's your excuse of choice when it comes to all of your behavior. But I don't buy it."

"My excuse?" he asked. "I'm glad to know you consider five years in prison to be an excuse."

"I'm just saying that if you know you're behaving badly you could probably behave *less badly*."

He snorted. "You have a lot of unearned opinions."

"Well, maybe help me earn some of them. Stop making pronouncements at me about how I don't know what I'm doing and help me figure out what I'm doing. We had sex. We can't change that. I don't want to change it."

"Faith…"

"I don't see why we can't…keep having sex. I'm designing a house for you. There's a natural end to our acquaintance. It's…" She laughed, shaking her head. "You know, when my brother Isaiah proposed to his wife he told her it made sense. That it was logical. And I was angry at him because it was the least romantic thing I'd ever heard."

"I'm not sure I follow you."

"They weren't dating. She was his assistant. He was looking for a wife, and because he thought she was such a good assistant it meant she would likely make a good wife."

"And that went well for him?"

"Well, not at first. And I was angry at him. I hated the fact that he was turning something personal into a rational numbers game. It didn't seem right. It didn't seem fair. But now it kind of makes sense to me. Not that we are talking about marriage, but…an arrangement. Being near each other is going to be difficult after what we shared."

"I'm fine," he lied, taking a step away from her and her far-too-earnest face.

If *fine* was existing in a bad mood with a persistent hard-on, yeah, he was fine.

"I'm not," she said softly.

She took a step toward him, just like she had done on those other occasions. Like a kid who kept reaching her hand toward the stove, even though she'd been burned.

That he thought of that metaphor should be the first clue he needed to take a step away. But he didn't.

It's too late.

The damage had already been done.

The time in prison had already changed him. Hell, maybe the damage had been done when he was born. His father's genes flowing through his veins were far too powerful for Levi to fight against.

"Until you're done designing the house," he said, his voice hard. "Just until then."

Her shoulders sagged in relief, and the look of vulnerability on her face would have made a better man rethink everything.

But Levi wasn't a better man. And he had no intention of attempting to be one at this point.

"I'm supposed to be at work," she said. "I really should get back."

He reached out and grabbed the handle on the front door, shutting it hard behind her. "No," he said. "Baby, you stepped into the lion's den. And you're not leaving until I'm good and ready for you to leave."

"But work," she said, her voice small.

"But this," he responded, wrapping his hand

around her wrist and dragging her palm toward him. He pressed it against that hard-on making itself known in the front of his jeans.

"Oh," she said, pressing her palm more firmly down and rubbing against him.

"You want to do this, we're doing it my way," he said. "I didn't know you were a virgin the first time, but now it's done. Taken care of. I'm not going to go easy on you just because you're inexperienced, do you understand?"

And he wasn't sure she had any idea at all what she was agreeing to. She nodded again.

If he was a better man, that, too, might have given him pause.

But he wasn't. So it didn't.

"I like to be in charge. And I don't have patience for inhibition. Do you understand me?" She looked up at him, those eyes wide. He didn't think she understood at all. "That means if you want to do it, you do it. If you want me to do it, you ask for it. Don't hide your body from me, and I won't hide mine from you. I want to see you. I want to touch you everywhere. And there's no limit to what I'm going to do. That means the same goes for you. You can do whatever you want to me."

"But you're in charge," she said faintly.

"And that's my rule. If you think it'll feel good, do it. For you, for me." He leaned in, cupping her head in his hand and looking at her intently. "Sex can be a chore. If you're in a relationship with someone for a long time and there's no spark between you anymore—which doesn't happen on accident, you have to stop caring—then it can be perfunctory. Lights off. Something you just do. Like eating dinner.

"Now, if there's no emotional divide I don't mind routine sex. There's a comfort in it. But I hadn't had sex in five years. There is no routine for me. That means I want raw. I want dirty. Because it can be that, too. It can be wild and intense. It can be slow and easy. It can be deliciously filthy. Sex can make you agree to things, say things, do things that if you were in your right mind you would find…objectionable. But when you're turned on, a lot of things seem like a good idea when they wouldn't otherwise. And that's the space I want to go to with you. That means no thinking. Just feeling."

Then he lifted her up and slung her over his shoulder. She squeaked, but she didn't fight his hold as he carried her out of the entry and up the stairs.

"You don't have your custom orgy bed yet."

He chuckled as they made their way down the hall, and he kicked open the door with his foot. "Well, we're not having an orgy, are we? This is a party for two."

"How pedestrian. It must be so boring for you."

"No talking, either."

He laid her down on the bed and she looked up at him, mutinous.

"Did you have a bra to wear today?"

"Yes."

"I have your other one."

She squinted. "I have more than one. I have more than *two*."

"Let me see this one."

She shifted, sat up and pulled her top over her head, exposing the red lace bra she had underneath. Then she reached behind herself, unzipped her pencil skirt and tugged it down, revealing her pair of matching panties.

"Damn," he said. "Last night, before we started, I'd planned on that side-of-the-road stuff being just the introduction."

"Yes, and then you got ridiculous."

"I *tried*," he said, his voice rough. "I tried not to be a monster, Faith. Because I might not have known you were a virgin, or at least I didn't admit it to myself, but I knew that…my hands are dirty. I'm just gonna get you dirty."

She looked up at him, and the confusion and hope in her eyes reached down inside him and twisted hard. "You said sex was fun when it was dirty."

"Different kinds of dirty, sweetheart."

She eased back, propping herself up on her forearms. It surprised him how bold she was, and suddenly, he wanted to know more. About this little enigma wrapped in red lace. An architectural genius. So advanced in so many ways, and so new in others.

"Take your bra and panties off," he commanded.

She reached back and unclipped her bra, pulling it off quickly. There was a slight hesitation when she hooked her thumbs in the waistband of her panties and started to pull them down. But only a slight one.

She wiggled out of them, throwing them onto the floor.

She kept the same position, lying back, not covering herself. Exposing her entire, gorgeous body.

Small, perfect breasts with pale pink nipples and a thatch of dark curls between her legs.

"I wanted to do the right thing. Just once. Even if I'd already done the wrong thing. But I give up, babe. I give the hell up."

He moved toward the edge of the bed, curved his arms up around her hips and dragged her toward him, pressing a kiss to her inner thigh. She made a small, kittenish sound as he moved farther down, nuzzled her center and then took a leisurely lick, like she was the finest dessert he'd ever encountered. She squirmed, squeaking as he held her more tightly, and he brought her fully against his face and began to devour her.

It had been so long. So long since he'd tasted a woman like this, and even then…

Faith was sweeter than anyone.

Faith wiped away the memory of any previous lover. Doing this for her was like a gift to himself.

He brought his hand between her legs and pressed two fingers deep inside her, working them in and out, in time with his tongue. He could feel her orgasm winding up tight inside of her. Could feel little shivers in her internal muscles, her body slippery with need. He drew out that slickness, rubbing two fingers over her clit before bringing his lips back down and sucking that bundle of nerves into his mouth as he plunged his fingers back in. She screamed, going stiff and coming hard, those muscles like a vise around his fingers now as her climax poured through her.

By the time she was finished, he was so damn hard he thought he was going to break in two.

He stood up, stripped his shirt over his head and came back down on the bed beside her.

She was looking at him with a kind of clouded wonder in her eyes, delicate fingertips tracing over the lines on his arms. "These are beautiful," she said.

"You want to talk about my tattoos now?"

"That was great," she said, breathless. "But I was waiting to see these."

"Celtic knot," he said, speaking of the intricate designs on his arms. That wasn't terribly personal. He'd had it done when he was eighteen and kind of an idiot. He'd hated his father and had wanted to find some identity beyond being that man's son. Inking some of his Irish heritage on his skin, making it about some long-dead ancestors, had seemed like a way to do that at the time.

Or at least that's what he'd told himself.

Now Levi figured it was mostly an attempt at looking like a badass and impressing women.

"And the bird?" she pressed.

Freedom. Simple as that. Also not something he was going to talk about with a hard-on.

"I like bird-watching," he said, his lips twitching slightly. "Now, no talking."

He gripped her chin and pulled her forward, kissing her mouth and letting her taste her own arousal there.

He took her deeper, higher, playing between her legs while he reached into his bedside table to get a condom.

Her head was thrown back, her breasts arched up toward him. Her lips, swollen from kissing, parted in pleasure. She was his every dirty dream, this sweet little angel.

He kept on teasing her, tormenting her with his fingers while he lifted the condom packet to his lips with his free hand and tore it with his teeth. Then he rolled it onto his length, slowly, taking his position against the entrance of her body.

She was so hot. So slick and ready for him. He couldn't resist the chance to tease them both just a little bit more.

He held himself firmly at the base and arched his hips forward, sliding through those sweet folds of hers, pushing down against her clit and reveling in her hoarse sound of pleasure.

He wasn't made for her. There was no doubt about that. He was hard, scarred and far too broken to ever be of any use to her. But as he pressed the thick head of his erection against her, as he slid into her tight heat, inch by agonizing inch, he wondered if she wasn't made for him.

She gasped, arching against him, this time not in pain. Not like the first time.

She held on to his shoulders, her fingertips digging into his skin as he thrust into her, pulling out slowly before pressing himself back home.

Again. And again.

Until they were both lost in the fog of pleasure. Until she was panting. Begging.

Until the only sound in the room was their bodies, slapping against each other, their breathing, harsh and broken. It was the middle of the day, and he hadn't taken her on a date. Hadn't given her anything but an orgasm. And he couldn't even feel guilty about it.

He had spent all those days in the dark. Counting the hours until nothing. Until the end. He had been given a life sentence. And with that there was almost no hope. Just a small possibility they'd find a body—as horrendous as that would be—and exonerate him. He had felt guilty hoping for that, even for a moment. But something. *Anything* to prove his innocence.

That had been his life. And he had been prepared for it to be the rest of his life.

And now, somehow, he was here. With her.

Inside Faith's body, the sunlight streaming in through the windows.

Blinded by the light, by his pleasure, by his need.

This was more than he had imagined having a chance to feel ever again. And he wasn't sure he'd ever felt anything like this. Like this heat and hunger that roared in his gut, through his veins.

He opened his eyes and looked at her, forced himself to continue watching her even as his orgasm burst through him like a flame.

It was like looking at hope.

Not just a sliver of it, but full and real. Possibilities he had never imagined could be there for him.

He had come from a jail cell and had intended to ask this woman to build a house for him, and instead…

They were screwing in the middle of the afternoon.

And something about it felt like the first real step toward freedom he'd taken since being released from prison.

She arched beneath him, gasping at her pleasure, her internal muscles gripping him as she came. He roared out his own release, grasping her tightly against his body as he slammed into her one last time.

And as he held her close against his chest, in a bed he should never have taken her to, he let go of the ideas of right and wrong. What she deserved. What he could give.

Because what had happened between them just now was like nothing he'd ever experienced on earth. And it wouldn't be forever. It couldn't be.

But if it was freedom for him, maybe it could be that for her, too.

Maybe…

Just for a little while, he could be something good for her.

And as he stared down at her lovely face, he ignored the hollow feeling in his chest that asked: Even if he knew he was bad for her, would he be able to turn away now?

He knew the answer.

He held her close, pressed her cheek against his chest, against his thundering heartbeat.

And she pressed her hand over the knife wound on his midsection.

Oh, yes. He knew the answer.

Nine

By the time Faith woke up, the sun was low in the sky, and she was wrapped around Levi, her hand splayed on his chest. He was not asleep.

"I was wondering when you might wake up."

She blinked sleepily. "What time is it?"

"About five o'clock."

"Shit!" She jerked, as if she was going to scramble out of bed, and then she fell back, laying down her head on his shoulder. "I'm supposed to have dinner with my parents tonight."

"What time?"

"Six. But Isaiah and Joshua are going to pester me about where I was. Poppy probably won't let me off, either. My sister-in-law. She works in the office. She's the one who—"

"Former assistant," Levi said.

"Yes. Also, she's pregnant right now and you know how pregnant women have a heightened sense of smell?" she asked.

"Um…"

"Well, she does. But I think more for shenanigans than anything else."

"Shenanigans?" he repeated, his tone incredulous. "Are we engaging in shenanigans?"

"You know what I mean," she huffed.

"When are you going to tell them?"

She blinked. "About…this?"

"Not this specifically," he said, waving his arm over the two of them to indicate their bodies. "But the design project. They're going to have to know eventually."

"Oh, do they?" She tapped her chin. "I was figuring I could engage in some kind of elaborate money-laundering situation and hide it from them forever."

"Well, that will impact on my ability to do a magazine spread with my new house. My new life as a nonconvict. As a free man."

"Right. I forgot."

"The best revenge is living well. Mostly because any other kind of revenge is probably going to land me back in prison."

"Isn't that like…double jeopardy at this point?"

"Are you encouraging me to commit murder?"

"Not encouraging you. I just… On a technicality…"

"I'm not going to do anything that results in a body count," he said drily. "Don't worry. But I would really like my ex to see everything I'm buying with the money that she can't have. If she can't end up in prison, then she's going to end up sad and alone, and with nothing. That might sound harsh to you…"

"It doesn't," Faith said, her voice small. "I can't imagine caring about someone like that and being betrayed. I can't imagine being in prison for five days, much less five years. She deserves…" She looked down, at his beautiful body, at the scar that marred his skin. "She deserves to think about it. What she could have had. What she gave away. Endlessly. She deserves that. I am so…sorry."

"I don't need your pity," he said.

"Just my body?" She wiggled closer to him, experimenting with the idea that she, too, could maybe be a vixen.

"I do like your body," he said slowly. "When are you going to tell your brothers about the job?"

"You know what? I'll do it tonight."

"Sounds pretty good. Do it when you have your parents to act as a buffer."

She grinned. "Basically."

She didn't want to leave him. Didn't want to leave this. She hesitated, holding the words in until her heart was pounding in her ears. Until she felt lightheaded.

"Levi… We have a limited amount of time together. It will only be until the design project is finished. And I don't want to go all clingy on you, but I would like to… Can I come back tonight?"

He sat up, swinging his legs over the side of the

bed, his bare back facing her. Without thinking, she reached out, tracing the border of the bird's wing that stretched around to his spine.

"Sure," he said. "If you really want to."

"For sex," she said. "But it might be late when we're finished. So maybe I'll sleep here?"

"If you want to sleep here, Faith, that's fine. Just don't get any ideas about it."

"I won't. I'll bring an overnight bag and I won't unpack it. My toothbrush will stay in my bag. It won't touch your sink."

"Why the hell would I care about that?"

He looked almost comically confused. On that hard, sculpted face, confusion was a strange sight.

"I don't know. There were some girls in college who used to talk about how guys got weird about toothbrushes. I've never had a boyfriend. I mean... Not that you're my boyfriend. But... I'm sorry. I'm speaking figuratively."

"Calm down," he said, gripping her chin and staring her right in the eyes. He dropped a kiss on her mouth, and instantly, she settled. "You don't need to work this hard with me. What we have is simple. We both know the rules, right?"

"Yes," she said breathlessly.

"Then I don't want you to overthink it. Because I definitely don't want you overthinking things when we're in bed together."

She felt a weight roll off her shoulders, and her entire body sagged. "Sometimes I think I don't know how to...not overthink."

"Why is that?"

She shrugged. "I've been doing it for most of my life."

He looked at her. Not moving. Like a predator poised to pounce. Those blue eyes were far too insightful for her liking. "Does it ever feel like prison?"

She frowned. "Does what ever feel like prison?"

"The success you have. You couldn't have imagined that you would be experiencing this kind of demand at your age."

"I really don't know how to answer that. Nobody sentenced me to anything, Levi, and I can walk away from it at any time."

"Is your family rich, Faith?"

She laughed. "No. We didn't grow up with anything. I only went to private school because I got a scholarship. Joshua didn't even get to go to college. He didn't have the grades to earn a scholarship or anything. My parents couldn't afford it—"

"All the money in your family—this entire company—it centers around you."

"Yes," she said softly.

He made a scoffing sound. "No wonder you were a virgin."

"What does my virginity have to do with anything?"

"Have you done something for yourself? Ever?"

"I mean, in fairness, Levi, it's my…gift. My talent. My dream, I guess, that made us successful. It centers around me. Isaiah and Joshua fill in the holes with what they do well, but they could do what they do well at any kind of company. The architectural aspect… That's me. They're enabling me to do what I love."

"And you're enabling everyone to benefit from your talents. That they're supporting your talent doesn't make them sacrificial. It makes them smart. I'm not putting your brothers down. In their position I would do the same. But what bears pointing out is that whether you realize it or not, you've gotten yourself stuck in the center of a spider's web, honey. No wonder you feel trapped sometimes."

They didn't speak about anything serious while she got ready. She dodged a whole lot of groping on his end while she tried to pull on her clothes, and ended up almost collapsing in a fit of giggles as she fought to get her skirt back on and cover her ass while he attempted to keep his hand on her body.

But she thought about what he said the entire time, and all the way over to her parents' house. His observation made it seem… Well, like she really should fight harder for the things she wanted. Should worry less about what Joshua and Isaiah felt about her association with Levi. Personally or professionally.

Though, she wasn't going to bring up any of the personal stuff.

Levi was right. The business, her career—all of this had turned into a monster she hadn't seen coming. It was a great monster. One that funded a lifestyle she had never imagined could be hers. Though, it was a lifestyle she was almost too busy to enjoy. And if that was going to be the case…

Why shouldn't she take on projects that interested her?

That was the thing. Levi had interested her from the beginning, and the only reason she had hesitated was because Joshua and Isaiah were going to be dicks about her interest and she knew it.

She pulled up to her parents' small, yellow farmhouse and sat in the driveway for a moment.

She wished Levi was with her. Although she had no reason to bring him. And the very idea of that large, hard man in this place seemed…impossible. Like a god coming down from Mount Olympus to hang out at the mall.

She got out of the car and walked up to the front porch, opened the door and walked straight inside. A rush of familiarity hit her, that familiar scent of her mother's pot roast. That deep sense of home that could only ever be attached to this place. Where she had grown up. Where she'd longed to be while at boarding school, where she had ached to return for Christmases, spring breaks and summers.

Everyone was already there. Devlin and his wife, Mia. Joshua, Danielle and their son Riley. Isaiah and Poppy.

Faith was the only one who stood alone. And suddenly, it didn't feel so familiar anymore.

Maybe because she was different.

Because she had left part of herself in that bed with Levi.

Or maybe because everyone else was a couple.

All she knew was that she felt like a half standing there and it was an entirely unpleasant feeling.

"Hi," Faith said.

"Where have you been?" Joshua asked. "You left the office around lunchtime the other day and I haven't seen you since."

"You say that like it's news to me," she said drily. "I had some things to take care of."

Her mom came out of the kitchen and wrapped Faith in a hug. "What things? What are you up to?" She pressed a kiss to Faith's cheek. "More brilliance?"

Her dad followed, giving Faith a hug and a kiss and moving to his favorite chair that put him at the head of the seating arrangement.

"I don't know." Faith rubbed her arm, suddenly feeling like she was fifteen and being asked to discuss her report card. "Not especially. Just… I picked up another project."

"What project?" Isaiah asked, frowning.

"You didn't consult me about the schedule first," Poppy said.

"I can handle it," Faith said. "It's fine."

"This is normally the kind of thing you consult us on," Joshua said, frowning.

"Yes. And I didn't this time. I took a job that interested me. And I had a feeling you wouldn't be very supportive about it. So I did it alone. And it's too late to quit, because I already have an agreement. I'm already working on the project, actually."

"Is that why you were behind on sending me those

estimates?" Isaiah asked. As if this error was proof positive they were actually correct, and she couldn't handle all this on her own.

"Yes," she said. "Probably. But, you know, I'm the one who does the design. And I should be able to take on projects that interest me. And turn down things that don't."

"Are we making you do things you don't like?"

"No. It's just… The whole mass-production thing we're doing, that's fine. But I don't need to be as involved in that. I did some basic designs, but my role in that is done. At this point it's standardized, and what interests me is the weird stuff. The imaginative stuff."

"I'm glad you enjoy that part of it. It's what makes you good. It's what got us where we are."

"I know. I mean…" Everyone was staring at her and she felt strange admitting how secure she was in her talent. But she wasn't a fifteen-year-old explaining a report card. She was a grown woman explaining what she wanted to do with the hours in her day, confident in her area of expertise. "You can't get where I'm at without being confident. But what I'm less confident about is whether or not you two are going to listen to me when I say I know what I want to do."

"Of course we listen to you."

She sucked in a sharp breath and faced down Joshua and Isaiah. "I took a design job for Levi Tucker."

Isaiah frowned. "Why do I know that name?"

It was Devlin who stood up, and crossed large, tattooed arms over his broad chest. "Because he's a convict," he said. "He was accused of murdering his wife."

"Who isn't dead," Faith pointed out. "So, I would suggest that's a pretty solid case *against* him being a murderer."

"Still."

Mia spoke tentatively. "I mean, the whole situation is so…suspicious, though," she said softly. "I mean…what woman would run from her husband if he was a good guy?"

"Yes," Faith said, sighing heavily, "I've heard that line of concern before. But the fact of the matter is, I've actually met him." She felt like she did a very valiant job of not choking on her tongue when she said that. "And he's…fine. I wouldn't say he's a nice guy, but certainly he's decent enough to work with."

"I don't like it," Devlin said. "I think you might be too young to fully understand all the implications."

Anger poured into her veins like a hot shot of whiskey, going straight to her head. "Do not give me that shit," she said, then looked quickly over at her mother and gave her an apologetic smile for the language. "Your wife is the same age as I am. So if I'm too young to make a business decision, your wife is certainly too young to be married to you."

Mia looked indignant for a moment, but then a little bit proud. The expression immediately melted into smugness.

"I like his ideas." Faith didn't say anything about

his house being a sex palace. "And it's a project I'm happy to have my name on."

Joshua shook his head. "You want to be associated with a guy like that? A young, powerful woman like yourself entering into a business agreement with a man who quite possibly has a history of violence against women…"

She exploded from the table, flinging her arms wide. "He hasn't done anything to anyone. There have been no accusations of domestic violence. He didn't… As far as anyone knows, he never did anything to her. She disappeared and he was accused of all manner of things with no solid evidence at all. And I think there was bias against him because he comes from…modest beginnings."

"It's about the optics, Faith," Joshua pointed out. "You're a role model. And associating with him could damage that."

Optics. That word made her feel like a creature in a zoo instead of a human. It made her feel like someone who was being made to perform, no matter her feelings.

"I don't care about *optics*, Joshua. I'm twenty-five years old and I have many more years left in this career. If all I ever do is worry about optics and I don't take projects that interest me—if I don't follow my passion even a little bit—then I don't see the point of it."

"The point is that you are going to be doing this for a long time and when you're more well-established you can take risks. Until then, you need to be more cautious."

She looked around the room at her family, all of them gazing at her like she had grown a second head. Suddenly she did feel what Levi had described earlier.

This was, in its way, a prison.

This success had grown bigger than she was.

"I'm not a child," she said. "If I'm old enough to be at the center of all this success, don't you think I should follow my instincts? If I…burn out because I feel trapped then I won't be able to do my best work. If I burn out, I won't be able to give you all those years of labor, Joshua."

"Nobody wants that," her mother said. "Nobody expects you to work blindly, Faith. No one wants you to go until you grind yourself into the ground." She directed those words at Joshua and Isaiah.

"You think it's a good idea for her to work with an ex-con?" Joshua directed *that* question at their father.

"I think Faith's instincts have gotten all of you this far and you shouldn't be so quick to dismiss them just because it doesn't make immediate sense to you," her father responded.

Right. This was why she had confessed in front of her parents. Because, while she wanted to please them, wanted all their sacrifices to feel worth it, she also knew they supported her no matter what. They were so good at that. So good at making her feel like her happiness mattered.

A lot of the pressure she felt was pressure she had put on herself.

But every year when there was stress about the scholarship money coming through for boarding school, every year when the cost of uniforms was an issue, when a school trip came up and her parents had to pay for part of it, and scraped and saved so Faith could have every opportunity… All of those things lived inside her.

She couldn't forget it.

They had done so much for her. They had set her out on a paved road to the future, rather than a dirt one, and it hadn't been a simple thing for them.

And she couldn't discount the ways her brothers had helped her passion for architecture and design become a moneymaking venture, too.

But at the end of the day, she was still owed something that was *hers*.

She still deserved to be treated like an adult.

It was that simple.

She just wanted them to recognize that she was a grown woman who was responsible for her own time, for her own decisions.

"I took the project," she said again. "It's nonnegotiable. He's going to publicize it whether you do or not, Joshua. Because it's part of his plan for… reestablishing himself. He's a businessman, and he was quite a famous one, for good reasons, prior to being wrongfully accused."

"Faith…" Joshua clearly sounded defeated now,

but he seemed to be clinging to a last hope that he could redirect her.

"You don't know him," Faith said. "You just decided he was guilty. Which is what the public did to him. What the justice system did to him. And if he's innocent, then he's a man who lost everything over snap judgments and bias. You're in PR, maybe you can work with that when the news stories start coming out—"

"Dinner will be ready soon," her mother interrupted, her tone gentle but firm. "Why don't we table talk of business until after?"

They did that as best they could all through the meal, and afterward Faith was recruited to help put away dishes. She would complain, or perhaps grumble about the sexism of it, but her mother had only asked for her, and Faith had a feeling it was because her mother wanted a private word with her.

"How well do you know Levi Tucker?" her mother asked gently, taking a clean plate from the drying rack and stacking it in the cupboard.

"Well enough," Faith answered, feeling a twist of conviction in her chest as she plunged her hands into the warm dishwater.

"You have very strong feelings about his innocence."

"There's nothing about him that seems…bad to me."

Rough, yes. Wounded, yes. Stabbed through the rib cage because of his own wife, sure. But not bad.

"Be careful," her mother said gently. "You've

seen more of the world than I ever will, sweetheart. You've done more, achieved more, than I could have ever hoped to. But there are some things you don't have experience with… And I fear that, to a degree, your advancement in other areas is the reason why. And it makes me worry for you."

"You don't have to worry for me."

"So your interest in him is entirely professional?"

Faith took a dish out of the soapy water and began to scrub it. "You don't have to worry about me."

"But I do," her mother said. "Just like I worry about your brothers sometimes. It's what parents do."

"Well, I'm fine," Faith said.

"It's okay to make mistakes," her mother said. "You know that, don't you?"

"What are you talking about?"

"Just forget about Levi Tucker for a second. It's okay for you to make mistakes, Faith. You don't have to be perfect. You don't have to be everything to everyone. You don't have to make Isaiah happy. You don't have to make Joshua happy. You certainly don't have to make your father and I happy."

Faith shifted uncomfortably. "It's not a hardship to care about whether or not my family is happy. You did so much for me…"

"Look at everything you've done for *us*. Just having you as my daughter would have been enough, Faith. It would have always been enough."

Faith didn't know why that sat so uncomfortably with her. "I would rather not make mistakes."

"We would all rather not make them," her mother

said. "But sometimes they're unavoidable. Sometimes you need to make them in order to grow into the person you were always supposed to be."

Faith wondered if Levi could be classified as a mistake. She was going into this—whatever it was—knowing exactly what kind of man he was and exactly when and how things were going to end. She wondered if that made her somehow more prepared. If that meant it was a calculated maneuver, rather than a mistake.

"I can see you, figuring out if you're still perfect."

Her mother's words were not spoken with any sort of unkindness, but they played at Faith's insides all the same. "I don't think I'm perfect," Faith mumbled, scrubbing more ferociously at the dish.

"You would like to be."

She made a sound that landed somewhere between a scoff and a laugh, aiming for cool and collected and achieving neither. "Who doesn't want to be?"

"I would venture to say your brothers don't worry very much about being perfect."

Sure. Because they operated in the background and worried about things like *her* optics, not their own. Isaiah somehow managed to go through life operating as if everything was a series of numbers and spreadsheets. Joshua treated everything like a PR opportunity. And Devlin... Well, Devlin was the one who had never cared what anyone thought. The one who hadn't gone into business with the rest of them. The one who had done absolutely everything on his own terms and somehow come out of it with Faith's best friend as a bonus.

"I like my life," Faith insisted. "Don't think that I don't."

"I don't think that," her mother said. "I just think you put an awful lot of pressure on yourself."

For the rest of the evening, Faith tried not to ruminate on that too much, but the words kept turning over and over in her head on the drive back to Levi's. She swung by her house and put together a toiletries bag, throwing in some pajamas and an outfit for the next day. And all the while she kept thinking…

You're too hard on yourself. You can make mistakes.

And her resistance to those words worried her more than she would like to admit.

Logically, she was completely all right with this thing with Levi being temporary. With it being a mistake, in many ways. But she was concerned that there was something deep inside her that believed it would become something different. That believed it might work out.

Beneath her practicality she was more of a dreamer than she wanted to acknowledge.

But how could she be anything but a dreamer? It was her job. To create things out of thin air. Even though another part of her always had to make those dreams a practical reality. It wasn't any good to be an architect if you couldn't figure out how to make your creations stand, make them structurally sound.

She didn't know how to reconcile those two halves of herself. Not right now. Not in this instance.

Now she had just confused herself. Because sex with Levi was not designing a house. Not even close.

She needed to stop trying to make sense of everything.

Maybe there were some things you couldn't make sense of.

She was having a just-physical relationship with the man. She nodded her head resolutely as she pulled up to the front of his house and put the car in Park. Then she shut off the engine decisively.

She knew exactly what was happening between them, and she was mature enough to cope with it.

He wasn't a mistake. He was an experience.

So there. She didn't need to make mistakes.

Satisfied with that, Faith grabbed her overnight bag, got out of her car and went to Levi's house.

Ten

Faith had only left his house once in the past two days. On Friday she went to work. But on Friday evening she returned, and stayed the night again. Now it was deep into Saturday, a gloomy, rainy day, and she was loitering around his kitchen wearing nothing but a T-shirt and a smile.

He didn't mind.

"I've got some horses coming later today," he commented, looking over at her lithe, pale form.

She hauled herself up onto the counter, the T-shirt riding up, nearly exposing that heaven between her thighs. She crossed those long, lovely legs at the ankles, her expression innocent, her hair disheveled from their recent activities.

The woman managed to look angelic and completely wicked all at once, and it did things to him he couldn't quite explain.

She wasn't for him. He had to remind himself. Because the things he liked about her... They didn't say anything good about him.

He had practically been born jaded. His vision of the world had been blackened along with his mother's eye the first time he had seen his father take his fists to her when he had been... He must've been two or three. His earliest memory.

Not a Christmas tree or his mother's smile. But her bruises. Fists connecting against flesh and bone.

That was his world. The way he had known and understood it from the very start.

He had never been able to see the world with the kind of unspoiled wonder Faith seemed to.

He had introduced her to dirty, carnal things, and had watched her face transform with awe every time he'd made her come. Every time he'd shown her something new, something illicit. She touched his body, his tattoos, his scars, like they were gifts for her to discover and explore.

There was something intoxicating in that.

This woman who saw him as *new*.

He had never had that experience with a woman before.

His high-school girlfriend had been as jaded and damaged as he was, and they might have experienced sex for the first time together, but there was no real wonder in it. Just oblivion. Just escape. The same way they had used drugs and alcohol to forget what was happening in their homes.

Sex with Faith wasn't a foggy escape. It was sharp and crisp like crystal, and just as able to cut him open. He had never felt so present, so in his own body, as he was when he was inside her.

He didn't know what the hell to make of it, but he didn't have the strength to turn away from it, either.

"Horses?"

"There's a small stable, and some arenas and pastures on this property. Of course, when I move to the other one…"

"You didn't tell me you needed a riding facility."

"I figured that's pretty standard, isn't it?"

"It doesn't have to be. It can be whatever you want it to be."

"Well, maybe I'll have you sketch that out for me, too."

"Can I meet the horses?" She looked bright and happy at the idea.

"Sure," he said. "You like to ride?"

"I never did as much of it as my brothers. I did a little bit when I was away at school, but I didn't spend as much time doing the farm-life thing as they did. I know how to ride, obviously. We always had a couple horses. It's just been a while. That was actually one of my brothers' priorities when we moved back here." She blinked. "You know, to get a ranching operation up and running."

He frowned. "Where do you live?"

She laughed. He realized that although the woman

designed houses for a living, they had never discussed her own living situation. "Okay. You know how they say contractors are notorious for never finishing the work in their own houses? Or how mechanics always have jacked-up cars? I am an architect who lives above a coffeehouse."

"No shit."

"None at all. It's too much pressure. Think of designing a place for myself. I haven't done it. I was living in this great, modern, all-glass space up in Seattle. And I loved it. But I knew that I wasn't going to stay there, so I didn't do anything else. When we moved back to Copper Ridge… I didn't really know what I wanted to do here, either. So I haven't designed a house. And the vacancy came up above The Grind in town and I figured an old building like that, all redbrick and right there in the center of things, was the perfect place for me to get inspiration. I was right. I love it. It works for me."

"That's disappointing. I thought you lived in some architectural marvel. Like something made entirely out of cement shaped like the inside of a conch shell."

"That's ridiculous."

"Is it?"

"Okay, it's not that insane. I've definitely seen weirder. How did you learn to ride?"

This was skating close to sharing. Close to subjects he didn't want to go into. He hesitated.

"I got a job on a ranch. I was a kid. Twelve. Thirteen. But it's what I did until I went away to school. Until I got into manufacturing. Until I made my for-

tune, I guess. There was an older guy, by the name
of Bud. He owned a big ranching spread on the edge
of Copper Ridge. He passed on a couple years ago
now. He took me on and let me work his land. He
was getting old, he was downsizing, but he didn't
have the heart to get rid of everything. So... I got to
escape my house and spend my days outdoors. Earn
a little money doing it. My grades suffered. But I
was damn happy.

"Ranch work will always be that for me. Freedom. It's one of the things I hated most about being
in prison. Being inside. Four walls around you all
the time. And... Nothing smells like a ranch does.
Like horses. Hay, wood chips. Even horse piss. It's its
own thing. That stuff gets in your blood. Not being
around it at all was like sensory deprivation. My assets were liquefied when I went to prison. Not frozen,
though, which was convenient for Alicia. Though,
in the end less convenient."

"Of course," she said testily.

"So, my horses were taken and sold, and the
money was put into an account. I was able to get
two of them back. They're coming today."

"Levi... That's... I mean... I can't believe you
lost your ranch? Your animals?"

"It doesn't matter."

"It does. She took... She took everything from
you." Faith blinked. "Do you think she did it on purpose?"

"I think she did," he said, his voice rough.

"Why? Look, I don't think that you did anything to her. But I…"

"The life I gave her wasn't the life she wanted," he said.

"Well, what life did she think she would be getting?"

"She—she was just like me. Poor and hating every minute of it. I was twenty-one. She was eighteen. She thought I might be on my way to something, and I swore to her I was. I thought she had hearts in her eyes, but they were just dollar signs. I loved her. We forged a path together, I thought. Were working toward a future where we could both look down on everyone who'd ever looked down on us."

"From a house on a hill?" Faith asked, softly.

"Yeah. From a house on a hill. But Alicia wanted more than that. She wanted to be something other than country, and I was never going to be that. Galas and all that crap. Designer clothes and eating tiny portions of food standing up and pretending to care about what strangers have to say about anything—it wasn't me. But I thought we were weathering those differences, I really did."

He shook his head. "When she went missing, it was the worst night of my life. She didn't take anything with her, not that I could see. I thought for sure something had happened to her. She had her purse, but that was it. It looked like she'd been snatched walking between a grocery store and her car. I lost sleep wondering what was happening to her. Dammit, I was picturing her being tortured. Violated.

Terrified. I've never been so afraid, so sick to my stomach, in my whole life. We might not have been in the best space right then, but I didn't want anything to happen to my wife, Faith. Hell, I didn't even think it was so bad that we would get divorced. I figured we needed to work on some things, but we could get around to it."

Faith bit her lip. "I can't imagine. I can't imagine what you went through."

"It was awful. And then they came and arrested me. Said they had reason to believe I'd done something to her. And later…that there was evidence I'd killed her and made sure the body wouldn't be found. The body. My wife was a body at that point. And they were accusing me of being responsible for that." He shook his head. "And what an ass I was. I grieved for her."

"Do you—do you think she ever loved you?" Faith asked. "I can't imagine doing that to someone I hated, much less—"

"I think she did in the beginning. But everything got twisted. She thought wealth and success meant something to me that it didn't. I wanted a ranch, and I wanted to go to fewer parties. I was fine with her going by herself. She didn't like that. She wanted me to be on her arm. She wanted a very specific life, and it was one she didn't inform me she wanted until it was too late. And I—"

"You weren't willing to give it."

He felt like he'd been punched in the chest.

Faith shrugged. "It's still no excuse to go framing you for murder," she said. "Or, whatever she intended to frame you for. But I just mean... There were maybe one or two things you could have given her to make her happier. If she wasn't a psycho."

He chuckled hollowly. "I expect you're right. If she weren't a psycho. But that's why I don't ever intend to get married again."

"Honestly, I can't blame you." Faith looked down, a dark curl falling into her face.

"Do you want to go for a ride later today?"

She looked at him, her whole face bright, her expression totally different from the way it had been a moment before. "Yes."

"Well, cowgirl, I hope you brought your jeans."

Eleven

Faith sat on the top of the fence while she watched the horses circle the paddock. They seemed content in their new surroundings. Or maybe, it was the presence of Levi. Watching as he had greeted the horses, pressing his hand to their velvet soft noses, letting them take in his scent had been…

Her chest felt so full she thought it might burst.

He was such a hard man. And yet… It was that hardness that made the soft moments so very special. She didn't know why she was thinking about him in those terms. Why she wanted special moments. Why she cared.

But seeing him like that, even now, out in the paddock, as the horses moved around him, and he stood in that black Stetson, black T-shirt and tight jeans…

She ached.

She had been outside of so many things. There, but not quite a part of them.

The only single person at dinner last night. A prodigy in architecture, but so much younger than everyone else, seemingly someone people couldn't relate to. The poor girl at boarding school, there on a scholarship. The smart kid who would rather escape into books and her imagination than go to a party.

That had been fine. It had been fine for a long time.

But it wasn't fine now.

She wanted to meld herself with him. Mold herself into his life. Melt against him completely. She didn't know what that meant. But the urge tugged at her, strongly. Made it so she could hardly breathe.

She hopped down off the fence, her boots kicking up dust as she made her way across the arena and toward him.

"What are you doing?" he asked.

"I just… They're beautiful horses." And he was beautiful. With them, he was stunning. It was like watching him be right where he belonged. At ease for the first time since she'd met him.

Like a bird spreading its wings.

A smile tipped up the corners of his lips. "I'm glad to have them back."

"The others?"

"It's not possible to track all of them down. It's okay. For now, this is enough."

"And then what?"

"They'll make a great story," he said, his expression suddenly shuttered. "When we do that big magazine spread. Showing my new custom home, and the equestrian facility you're going to build me. A big picture of me with these horses that Alicia took from me."

"Is that what everything is about?"

"My entire life has been about her for seventeen years, Faith. In the last five years of that all I could do was think about…" He gritted his teeth. "That is the worst part. I worried about her. All that time. And she was fine. Off sipping champagne and sitting on a yacht. Screwing who the hell knows. While I sat in prison like a monk. An entire life sentence ahead of me. And I was worried about her. She knew I was in prison. She knew. She didn't care. That's the worst part. How much emotional energy I wasted worrying about the fate of that woman when…"

She stepped forward, put her fingertips on his forearm. "This isn't emotional energy?"

He looked down at her. "How would you feel? How would you feel in my position?"

"I don't know. Possibly not any better. I don't know what I would do. You're right. I can't comment on it."

"Stick to what you do, honey. Comment on the design work you can do for me."

She took a step back, feeling like she had overstepped. That little bubble of fantasy she'd had earlier, that need to get closer to him, had changed on her now. "I will. Don't worry."

"How did you realize you were an architecture prodigy?" he asked suddenly.

"I don't know," she said, lifting a shoulder. "I mean, I drew buildings. I was attracted to the idea of doing city design in a slightly more…organic way. I was fascinated by that from the time I was a kid. As for realizing I was good… I was naturally good at art, but I've always been good at math and science as well. History. Art history."

"So you're one of those obnoxious people who doesn't have a weakness."

"Well, except for…social stuff?" She laughed. "Academically, no. Not so much. And that opened a lot of doors for me. For which I will always be grateful. It was really my brothers who helped me focus. Because, of course, Isaiah being a numbers guy, he wanted to help me figure out how I could take what I did and make money with it. My education was paid for because I was brilliant, but that comes to an end eventually. You have to figure out what to do in the real world. Architecture made sense."

"I guess so."

"Why…manufacturing? And what did you make?"

"Farm equipment," he said. "Little generic replacement parts for different things. A way to do it cheaper, without compromising on quality."

"And what made you do that?"

"Not because I'm an artist. Because there are a lot of hardworking men out there, pleased as hell to replace the parts themselves if they can. But often things are overcomplicated and expensive. I wanted to find a way to simplify processes. So it started with the basic idea that we can get around some of the proprietary stuff some of the big companies did. And it went from there. Eventually I started manufacturing parts for those big companies. It's a tricky thing to accomplish, here in the United States, but we've managed. And it served me well to keep it here. It's become part of why my equipment is sought after."

She giggled. "There's a double entendre."

"It's boring. That was another thing my wife objected to. She wanted me to get into real-estate investing. Something more interesting for her to talk about with her friends. Something a little bit sexier than gaskets."

"A gasket is pretty sexy if it's paying you millions of dollars, I would think."

"Hell, that was my feeling." He sighed heavily. "It's not like you. Mine was a simple idea."

"Sometimes simplicity is the better solution," she said. "People think you need to be complicated to be interesting. I don't always think that's true, in design, or in life. Obviously, in your case, the simple solution was the revolutionary one."

"I guess so. Are you ready to go for a ride?"

"I am," she said.

And somehow, she felt closer to him. Somehow she felt…part of this. Part of him.

She wanted to hold on to that feeling for as long as it would last, because she had a feeling it would be over a lot sooner than she would like.

But then, that was true of all of this. Of everything with him.

She was beginning to suspect that nothing short of a lifetime would be enough with Levi Tucker.

Twelve

Levi had missed this. He couldn't pretend otherwise. Couldn't pretend that it hadn't eaten at him, five years away from the ranch.

The animals were in his blood, in his bones. Had been ever since he had taken that job at Bud's ranch. That experience had changed him. Given him hope for the future. Allowed him to see things in a different way. Allowed him to see something other than a life filled with pain, fear.

The other kids at school had always avoided him. He was the boy who came to school with bruises on his face. The boy whose family was whispered about. Whose mother always looked sallow and unhappy, and whose father was only ever seen at night, being pulled drunkenly out of bars.

But the horses had never seen him that way. He had earned their trust. And he had never taken it for granted.

The back of a horse was the one place he had ever felt like he truly belonged. And things hadn't changed much. Twenty-three years—five of them spent behind bars—later, and things hadn't changed much.

He looked back from his position on the horse, and the grin on Faith's face lit up all the dark places inside him. He hadn't expected to enjoy sharing this with her. But then, he hadn't expected to share so much with her at all.

There was something about her. It was that sense of innocence.

That sense of newness.

A sense that if he could be close enough to her he might be able to see the world the way she did. As a place full of possibility, rather than a place full of pain. Betrayal. Heartbreak.

Yes, with her, he could see the scope of so much more. And it made him want to reach out to her. It made him want to…

He wanted her to understand him.

He couldn't remember ever feeling that way before. He hadn't wanted Alicia to understand him.

He hadn't cared. He'd loved her. But that love had been wrapped up in the life he wanted to build. In the vision of what they could be. He'd been focused on forward motion, not existing in the moment.

And maybe, there, Faith was right. Maybe that was where he had failed as a husband.

Though, he still hadn't failed so spectacularly that he'd deserved to be sent to prison, but he could acknowledge that some of the unhappiness in his marriage had come down to him.

"It's beautiful out here," Faith said.

"This is actually part of the property for the new house," he said. He glanced up at the sky, where the dark gray clouds were beginning to gather, hanging low. "It's starting to look stormy, but if you don't mind taking a chance on getting caught in the rain, I can show you where we might put the equestrian facility."

"I'd like that," she said.

He urged his horse on, marveling at how quickly he had readjusted to this thing, to horsemanship, to feeling a deep brightness in his bones. If that wasn't evidence this was where he belonged, in the woods on the back of a horse, he didn't know what was.

They came through a deep, dark copse of trees and out into a clearing. The clouds there were layers of patchwork gray, moving from silver to a kind of menacing charcoal, like a closed fist ready to rain down judgment on the world below.

And there was the clearing. Overlooking the valley below.

The exact positioning he wanted, so he could look down on everyone who had once looked down on him.

"You think you can work with this?" he asked.

"Definitely," she responded. She maneuvered her horse around so she was more fully facing the view before them. "I want to make it mirror your house somehow. Functional, obviously. But open. I know the horses weren't in prison for the last five years, but they had their lives stolen from them, too, in a way. I want it all connected. And I want you to feel free."

Interesting that she had used that word. A word that had meant so much to him. One he had yearned for so much he'd traded cigarettes to have a symbol of it tattooed on his body.

It was a symbol he was deeply protective of. He wasn't a sentimental man, and his tattoos were about the closest thing to sentiment he possessed.

"I like the way you think," he said.

He meant it. In many ways. And not just this instance.

She tilted her head, scrunching her nose and regarding him like he was something strange and fascinating. "Why do you like the way I think?"

"Because you see more than walls, Faith. You see what they can mean to people. Not just the structure. But what makes people feel. Four walls can be a prison sentence or they can be a refuge. That difference is something I never fully appreciated until I was sent away."

"Homes are interesting," she said. "I design a lot of buildings that aren't homes. And in those cases, I design the buildings based on the skyline of the city. The ways I want the structure to flow with the surroundings. But homes are different. My parents' house, small and simple as it is, could not feel more like home to me. Nothing else will ever feel like home in quite the same way it does. It's where I grew up.

Where the essential pieces of myself were formed and made. That's what a home is. And every home you live in after those formative years…is not the same. So you have to try to take something from the life experience people have had since they left their parents and bring it all in and create a home from that."

He thought of his own childhood home. Of the way he had felt there. The fear. The stale scent of alcohol and sadness. The constant lingering threat of violence.

"Home to me was the back of a horse," he said. "The mountains. The trees. The sky. That's where I was made. It's where I became a person I could be proud of, or at the very least, a person I could live with. My parents' place was prison."

He urged his horse forward, moving farther down the trail, into the clearing, before he looped around and headed back toward the other property. Faith followed after him.

And the sky opened up. That angry fist released its hold.

He urged the horse into a canter, and he could hear Faith keeping pace behind him. As they rode, the rain soaked through his clothes. All the way through to his skin. It poured down his face, down his shirt collar.

Rain.

It had been five years since he had felt rain on his skin.

Fuck.

He hadn't even known he'd missed it until now.

And now he realized he was so thirsty for it he thought he might have been on the brink of death.

He released his hold on the reins and let his arms fall to his sides, spread his hands wide, keeping his body movements in tune with the horse as the water washed over him.

For a moment. Then two.

He counted the raindrops at first. Until it all blended together, a baptism out there in the wilderness.

He finally took control of the animal again. By then, the barn was back in view.

The horse moved with him as Levi encouraged him into a gallop. The rain whipped into his eyes now, but he didn't care. He brought the horse into the stable and looped the lead rope around a hook, then moved back outside and stripped off his shirt, letting the rain fall on his skin there, too.

If Faith thought it was strange, she didn't say anything. She went into the barn behind him and disappeared for a few moments. Leaving him outside, with the water washing over him. When she returned she was without her horse, her chin-length dark hair wet and clinging to her face.

"Are you okay?" she asked.

"I just realized," he said, looking up above, letting the water drops hit him square on the face. "I just realized that it's the first time I've felt the rain since before I was in jail."

Neither of them said anything. She simply closed

the distance between them and curved her fingers around his forearm.

They stood there for a while, getting wet together.

"Tell me about your family," she said softly.

"You don't want to hear the story."

"I do," she said.

"Maybe I don't feel like telling it," he responded, turning to face her.

She looked all around them, back up at the sky, and then back at him. "We're home," she said. "It's the best place to tell hard stories."

And he knew exactly what she meant. They were home. They were free. Outside and with no walls around them. In the exact kind of place he had found freedom for himself the first time.

"My very first memory is of my father hitting my mother in the face," he said. "I remember a bruise blooming there almost instantly. Blood. Tears. My home never felt safe. I never had that image of my father as a protector. My father was the enemy. He was a brutal man. He lived mean, and he died mean, and I've never mourned him. Not one day."

"How did he die?" she asked softly.

"Liver failure," he said. "Which is kind of a mundane way to die for a man like him. In some ways, it would've been better if he'd died in violence. But sometimes I take comfort in the fact that disease doesn't just come for good people. Sometimes it gets the right ones."

"Your mother?"

"Packed up and left Oregon the minute he died. I send her money sometimes. At least, I did before…"

"Obviously you couldn't send money when you were in prison."

He shook his head. "No. I don't think you understand. She didn't want anything from me after that. She didn't believe me. That I didn't have something to do with Alicia's disappearance. She figured I was cut from the same cloth as my old man."

"How could she think that?" Faith asked. "She was your mother."

"In the end, she was a woman standing with another woman. And part of me can't blame her for that. I think it was easier for her to believe that her worst nightmare had come true. That I had fully become the creation of my genetics. You can understand why she would have feared that."

He had feared it, too. Sometimes he still did.

Because that hate—that hard, heavy fist of rage living in his chest—felt far too evil to have been put there recently. It felt born into him. As much a part of him as that first memory.

He swept her up into his arms then and carried her toward the house, holding her tightly against his chest. She clung to him, her fingers slick against his skin, greedy as they trailed over him.

"That's who I am," he said, taking her hand and pressing it against the scar left by the knife. "And that's why I told you I wasn't the right man for you. That's why I told you to stay away from me."

She shifted her hand, moving her fingertips along

the scarred, raised flesh. The evidence of the day he'd been cut open and left to bleed. He'd considered lying down and dying. A damn low moment. He had been sentenced to life in prison, he'd thought. Why not let that sentence be a little shorter?

But his instincts, his body, hadn't let him give up. No. He'd gotten back up. And hit the man who'd come after him. And then hit him again, and again.

No one had come for Levi after that.

She made a soft sound as she shifted, letting her fingers glide over to the edge of the bird's wing. She traced the shape, its whole wingspan.

"No," she said, shaking her head. "*This* is who you are. This," she said. "This scar… You didn't choose that. You didn't choose to be born into a life of violence. You didn't choose your father. You didn't choose that time in prison. Didn't choose to get in a fight that day and have your body cut open. You chose *this*. These wings. This design. Whatever it means to you, you chose that. And it's more real than anything that was inflicted on you could ever be."

He stopped her from talking then, captured her mouth with his and silenced her with the fierceness of his kiss.

He wanted everything she said to be real. He wanted her words to matter, as much as everything that had come before them. As much as every blow he'd witnessed, every blow he'd been subjected to, every vile insult.

He wanted her kiss to mean more than his past.

He smoothed his hands down her body, his touch filled with reverence, filled with awe.

This woman, so beautiful and sweet, would touch *him*. Would give herself to *him*.

Yes, he wanted to believe what she said. He did. But he could see no way to do that. Couldn't find it in himself.

He could only be glad that somehow, he had found her.

He wanted to drown in her, as much as he had wanted to drown in the rain. To feel renewed. Clean. If only for a moment. She was like that spring rain. Restorative. Redemptive. More than he deserved, and essential in ways he wouldn't let himself think about.

She moved her hands over his body, over his face, pressing kisses to the scar on his ribs, to the tattoo, lower. Until she took him into her mouth, her tongue swirling in a torturous pattern over the swollen head of his erection. He bucked up, gripping her hair even as a protest escaped his lips.

"Let me," she said softly.

And then she returned her attention to him, this beautiful woman who had never done this for a man before. She lavished him with the kind of attention he didn't deserve, not from anyone, least of all her.

But he wanted it, wanted her. He wanted this in a way he hadn't wanted anything for longer than he could remember. He *wanted*, and it was because of her.

He *wanted*, and he would never forget her for it.

He *wanted*, and he would never forgive her for it.

She was hope. She was a promise of redemption he could never truly have.

She was *faith*, that's what she was. Believing in something you couldn't see or control. Until now, he had never wanted any part of something like that.

But here he was, drowning in it. In her.

A missing piece. To his life.

To his heart.

His vision began to blur, his body shaking, wracked with the need for release as Faith used her hands and her mouth on him. As she tempted him far beyond what he could handle.

He looked down at her, and their eyes met. He saw desire. Need.

And trust.

She trusted him. This beautiful angel trusted him like no one ever had.

And it pushed him right over the edge.

He didn't pull away from her, and she didn't stop, swallowing down his release before moving up to his mouth again, scattering kisses over his abs and his chest as she went. He claimed her lips, pressing his hands between her thighs, smoothing his fingers over her clit and pushing two deep inside her as he brought her to her own climax.

She clung to him, looking dazed, filled with wonder.

Yet again, because of him. She was a gift. Possibly the only gift he'd ever been given in all his life.

But Faith should have been a gift for another man. A man who knew how to treasure her.

Levi didn't know how to do that.

But he knew how to hold on.

She clung to him, breathing hard, her fingernails digging into his shoulders. "I don't want to go home," she said softly.

"Then stay with me."

She looked up at him, her face questioning.

"Yes," he confirmed. "Stay with me."

Thirteen

It was easy to let time slowly slip by, spending it in a bubble with Levi. It was a lot less easy for Faith to hide where she was spending all her nights and, frankly, half her days. If her brothers weren't suspicious of her behavior, Poppy certainly was.

There was no way she could get her unusual comings and goings past the eagle eye of her sister-in-law, and Poppy was starting to give Faith some serious side eye whenever Faith came into the office late, or left a little early.

Faith knew the reckoning was coming. She was going to have to deal with whatever was between her and Levi, and soon. Because the fact of the matter was, whatever they had agreed on in the beginning, she no longer wanted this relationship to be temporary.

The two of them had lapsed into a perfect routine over the past few weeks. When she wasn't at work, she was at his house, and often sketching.

Working sometimes late into the night while she watched him sleep, more and more ideas flowing through her mind.

She had begun to think of his new house like a bird's nest.

To go with the bird that he'd tattooed on his body. A place for that soaring creature to call home. A home that rested effortlessly in the natural environment around it, and seemed to be made from the materials of the earth.

Of course, maybe she was pondering all of that to the detriment of her other work. And that was a problem. She felt…so removed from her life right now. From everything she was supposed to care about.

She cared about Levi.

About what lay on the other side of all of this. About the changes taking place inside of her.

She should care more about her upcoming interview with *Architectural Digest*. She should care more about a television spot she was soon going to be filming in the office. One that was intended as a way to boost the participation of young girls in male-dominated fields, like architecture.

Instead, Faith was fixating on her boyfriend.

Immediately, her heart fell.

He wasn't her boyfriend. He was a man she had a temporary arrangement with, and she was becoming obsessed. She was becoming preoccupied.

Even so, she wasn't sure she cared. Because she had never been preoccupied in her life. She had always been focused, on task. Maybe it was her turn to go off the trail for a little while.

Maybe it was okay.

You don't have to be perfect.

Her mother's words rang in her ears, even as Faith sat there at her desk. She wasn't sure what perfect even looked like for her anymore and the realization left her feeling rocked.

Poppy was going to appear in a moment to film the television spot they were sending in, and Faith knew she needed to pull herself together.

She wasn't sure if she could.

The door cracked open and Poppy came in, a smile on her perfectly made-up face, her figure—and her growing baby bump—highlighted by the adorable retro wiggle dress she was wearing.

Poppy was always immaculate. The only time she had ever seemed frazzled in any regard was when she had been dealing with issues in her relationship with Isaiah. So maybe—*maybe*—Poppy would be the ally Faith needed.

Or at the very least, maybe she would be the person Faith could confide in. For all that they had married older men with their own issues, Hayley and Mia did not seem like they would be sympathetic to Faith's situation.

It was all very "do as I say and do" not "do the kind of man that I do."

"Are you ready?" Poppy asked.

Her skeptical expression said that she thought Faith was not ready. Though, Faith wasn't sure why Poppy felt that way.

"I was going to say yes," Faith said slowly. "But you clearly don't think so."

Poppy frowned. "You look very pale."

"I *am* pale," Faith said drily.

"Well," Poppy said, patting her own glowing, decidedly *not* pale complexion, "compared to some, yes. But that isn't what I meant. You need some blush. And lipstick with a color. I don't support this millennial pink nonsense that makes your lips blend into the rest of your skin."

"I'm *not* wearing lipstick."

"Well, there's your problem."

Poppy opened the drawer where Faith normally kept her makeup, and that was when Faith realized her mistake. The makeup wasn't there. Because she had taken the bag over to Levi's.

Poppy narrowed her eyes. "Where is your makeup?"

Faith tapped her fingers on her desk. "Somewhere?"

"Honestly, Faith, I wouldn't have been suspicious, except that was a dumbass answer."

"It's at Levi Tucker's," Faith said, deciding right in that moment that bold and brazen was what she would go for.

Everything was muddled inside her in part because she hadn't been sure if she wanted to go all in here. Cash her chips in on this one, big terrible thing that might be the mistake to end all mistakes.

But she did. She wanted to.

She wanted to go all in on Levi.

That horrible ex-wife of his had done that. She had cashed in all her chips on a moment when she could take his money and have the life she wanted with absolutely no care about what it did to him.

Well, why couldn't Faith do the opposite? Blow her life up for him. Why couldn't she risk herself for him?

No one in his life ever had. Not his father, who was drunk and useless and evil. Not his mother, who had allowed the scars and pains from her past to blind her to her own son's innocence.

Not his wife, who had been so poisoned by selfishness.

And Faith… What would she be protecting if she didn't?

Her own sense of perfection. Of not having let anyone down.

None of that mattered. None of it was *him*.

"Because you were…working on a job?" Poppy asked, her expression skeptical, but a little hopeful.

Faith's lips twitched.

"Some kind of job," she responded, intentionally digging into the double entendre, intentionally meeting Poppy's gaze. "So, there you have it."

"Faith…" Poppy said. "I don't… With a *client*?"

"I know," Faith said. "I didn't plan for it to go that

way. But it did. And… I only meant for it to be temporary. That's all. But… I love him."

The moment she said it, she knew it was true. All her life she had been apart. All her life she had been separate. But in his arms, she belonged. With him, she had found something in herself she had never even known was missing.

"Your brothers…"

"They're going to be mad. And they're going to be afraid I'll get hurt. I know. I'm afraid I'll get hurt. Which is actually why I said something to you. Isaiah is not an easy man."

Poppy at least laughed at that. "No," she said. "He isn't."

"He's worth it, isn't he?"

Poppy breathed out slowly, then took a few steps toward Faith's desk, sympathy and understanding crinkling her forehead. "Faith, I've loved your brother for more than ten years. And he was worth it all that time, even when he was in love with someone else."

"Levi's not in love with anyone else. But he's… angry. I'm not sure if there's any room inside him for any other emotion. I don't know if he can let it go."

"Have you told him that you love him?"

"No. You're the first person I've told."

"Why me?" Poppy asked.

"Well, first of all," Faith said, "Isaiah won't kill you."

"No," Poppy said.

"Second of all… I need to know what I should do.

Because I've never loved anyone before and I'm terrified. And I don't want him to be a mistake, and that has nothing to do with wanting to be perfect. And everything to do with wanting him. I'm not hiding it anymore. I'm not."

"You never had to hide it. No one needed you to be perfect."

"Maybe I needed it. I can't let them down." Faith shook her head. "I can't let them down, Poppy. Isaiah and Joshua have poured everything into our business. I can't… I can't mess up."

"They would never look at it that way," Poppy said. "Isaiah loves you. So much. I know it's hard for him to show it."

"It's easy for me to forget that he struggles, too. He seems confident."

"He is," Poppy said. "To his detriment sometimes. But he's also just human. A man who fell in love. When he didn't see it coming. So, he's not going to throw stones at you for doing the same."

"They're going to be angry about who it is. Levi's older than they are."

Poppy shook her head. "And Isaiah is my foster sister's ex-fiancé. We all have reasons things shouldn't be. But they are. And sometimes you can't fight it. Love doesn't ask permission. Love gets in the cracks. And it expands. And it finds us sometimes when we least expect it."

"So, you don't judge me?"

"I'm going to judge you if you don't put on some lipstick for the video. But I'm not going to judge you for falling in love with a difficult man who may or may not have the capacity to love you. Because I've been there."

"And it worked out."

"Yes," Poppy said, putting her hand on her stomach. "It worked out."

"And if it hadn't?" Faith asked.

Poppy seemed to consider that for a while, her flawlessly lipsticked mouth contorting. "If it hadn't, it would have still been worth it. In my case, I would still have the baby. And she would be worth it. But also… No matter what Isaiah was able to feel for me in the end, I never would have regretted loving him. In a perfect world, he would have always loved me. But the world isn't perfect. It's broken. I suspect it's that way for your Levi, too."

Faith nodded. "I guess the only question is… whether or not he's too broken to heal."

"And you won't know that unless you try."

"That sounds an awful lot like risk."

"It is. But love is like that. It's big, Faith. And you can't hold on to fear. Not if you expect to carry around something so big and important as love. Now get some lipstick on."

Fourteen

She was finished designing the house.

That day had been inevitable from the beginning. It was what they had been moving toward. It was, in fact, the point. But still, now that the day had arrived, Levi found himself reluctant to let go. He found himself trying to figure out ways he might convince her to stay. And then he questioned why he wanted that.

The entire point of hiring her, building this house, had been to establish himself in a new life. To put himself on a new path. The point had not been to get attached to his little architect.

He was on the verge of getting everything he wanted. Everything he needed.

She should have nothing to do with that.

And yet, he found himself fantasizing about bringing her into his home. Laying her down on that custom bed he didn't really want or need.

He hadn't seen the designs yet. In fact, part of him wanted to delay because after he approved the designs, Jonathan Bear would begin work on the construction aspects of the job. Likely, any further communications on the design would be between her and Jonathan.

Levi should be grateful that once this ended, it would end cold like that. For her sake.

He wasn't.

It was a Sunday afternoon, and he knew that meant she had dinner with her parents later. But she hadn't left yet. In fact, she was currently lying across the end of his bed, completely naked. She was on her stomach, with her legs bent at the knees and crossed at the ankles, held up in the air, kicking back and forth. Her hair had fallen in her face as she sketched earnestly, full lips pursed into a delicious O that made him think of how she'd wrapped them around his body only an hour or so earlier.

"Don't you have to be at your parents' place soon?" he asked.

She looked over at him, her expression enigmatic. "Yes."

"But?" he pressed.

"I didn't say 'but.'"

"You didn't have to," he said, moving closer to the bed and bringing his hands down on her actual butt with a smack. "I heard it all the same."

"Your concern is touching," she said, shooting

him the evil eye and rolling away from him. "It's complicated."

"I understand complicated family." He just didn't want to talk about complicated family. He wanted to get his hands all over her body again. But he could listen to her. For a few minutes.

"No," she corrected. "You understand irredeemable, horrendous families. Mine is just complicated."

"Are you going to skip this week?"

"Why do you care?"

It was a good question. Whether or not she went to her family's weekly gathering was only his concern if it impacted his ability to make love with her.

Right. Because making love is what she's been doing all day, every day at your house.

Not living together. Not playing at domesticity.

Going out and riding on the trails. Cooking dinner. Eating dinner. Going to sleep, waking up, showering.

Hell, they had ended up brushing their teeth together.

He could suddenly see why—per her earlier concern—men got weird about toothbrushes.

There was something intimate about a toothbrush.

There was also something about knowing her so intimately that made the sex better. Everything that made the sex unique to her made it better. Living with her, being near her, was foreplay.

He didn't have to understand it to feel it.

Faith cleared her throat. "I told Poppy about us."

He sat down on the edge of the bed. "Why?" He

had never met Poppy, but he knew all about her. Knew that she had pretty recently become Faith's sister-in-law. But he hadn't gotten the impression they were friends in particular.

"It just kind of…came out." She shrugged, her bare breasts rising and falling. For the moment, he was too distracted to think about what she was saying. "And I didn't see the point in hiding it anymore."

"I thought you really didn't want your brothers to know."

"I didn't. But now…"

"You finished designing the house. We both know that."

She ducked her head. "I haven't shown it to you yet."

"That doesn't change the fact that you're done. Does it?"

"I guess not. It's not a coincidence that I went ahead and told her now. I needed to talk to her about some things."

"Don't you think that if it's about—" he hesitated over saying the word *us* "—this, that you should have talked to me?"

"Yes, I do need to talk to you." She folded her knees upward, pushing herself into a sitting position. "I just… I needed to get my head on straight."

"And?"

"I failed. So, this is the thing." She frowned, her eyebrows drawing tightly together. "I don't want us to be over."

Her words hit him with all the force of a blade slipping into his rib cage.

"Is that so?"

He didn't want it to be over, either.

That was the thing. *Not being over* was what he had been pondering just a few moments ago. They didn't have to be over yet.

He almost felt as if everything else was on pause. His revenge, his triumphant return back into Alicia's circles. His determination to make sure that she went to prison by proving what she had done to him.

All of that ugliness could wait. It would have to. It was going to start once the house was finished. And until then…

What was the harm of staying with Faith?

Right. Her brothers know. Soon, her parents will know. And you really want all of that to come down on you?

That's not simple. That's not casual.

That's complicated.

But still. The idea that he could have her, for a little while longer. That he could keep her, locked away with him…

It was intoxicating.

"You want more of this?" he asked, trailing his finger along her collarbone, down her rib cage, then skimming over her sensitized nipple.

"Yes," she said, her voice a husky whisper. "But not just more of this. Levi, you have to know… You have to know."

Her eyes shone with emotion, with conviction.

His chest froze, his heart a block of ice. He couldn't breathe around it.

"I have to know what, little girl?" he asked, locking his jaw tight.

"How much I love you."

That wasn't just a single knife blade. That was an outright attack. Stabbing straight through to his heart and leaving him to bleed.

"What?"

"I love you," she said. She shook her head. "I didn't want it to be like this. I didn't want to be a cliché. I didn't want to be who you were afraid I would be. The virgin who fell for the first man she slept with. But I realized something. I'm not a cliché. I'm not a virgin who fell for the first man she slept with. I'm a woman who waited until she found something powerful enough to act on. Our connection came before sex. And I have to trust that. I have to trust myself. Until now, everything I've done has been safe."

"You went away to boarding school. You have excelled in your profession before the age of thirty. How can you call any of that safe?"

She clasped her hands in front of her, picking at her fingernails. "Because it made everyone happy. Not only that—for the most part, it made me happy. It was the path of least resistance. And it still is. I could walk away from you, and I could continue on with my plan. No love. No marriage. Until I'm thirty-five, maybe. Until I've had more of a career than many people have in a lifetime. Until I've done everything in the perfect order. Until I'm a triumph to my brothers and an achievement to my parents. It will make me feel proud, but it will never make me...*feel*. Not really.

"A career isn't who you are. It can't be. You know that. Everything you accomplished turned to dust because of what your ex did to you. She destroyed it, because those things are so easily destroyed. When everything burns there's one thing that's left, Levi. And that's the love of other people."

"You're wrong about that," he said, his chest tightening into a knot. "There is something else that remains through the fire. That's hatred. Blinding, burning hatred, and I have enough of that for two men. I have too much of it, Faith. Sometimes I think I might have been born with it. And until I make that bitch pay for what she did to me, that's how it's going to be."

"I don't understand what that has to do with anything."

Of course she didn't understand. Because she couldn't fathom the kind of rage and darkness that lived inside him. She had never touched a fire that burned so hot. Had never been exposed to something so ugly.

Until now. Until him.

"Then choose something else," she said. "Choose a different way."

"I've never had a choice," he said. "Ever. My fate was decided for me before I ever took a breath in this world."

"I don't believe that. If people can't choose, what

does that mean for me? Have I worked hard at any of this, or was it just handed to me? Did I ever have a choice?"

"That's different."

"Why?" she pressed. "Because it's about you, so that means you can see it however you want? You can't see how hypocritical that is?"

"Hypocrisy is the least of my concerns," he said.

"What *is* your concern, then? Because it certainly isn't me."

"That's where you're wrong. I warned you. I told you what this could be and what it couldn't be. You didn't listen."

"It wasn't a matter of listening. I fell in love with you by being with you. Your beauty is in everything you do, Levi. The way you touch me. The way you look at me."

"What's love to you?" he asked. "Do you think it's living here in this house with me? Do you think it's the two of us making love and laughing, and not dealing with the real world at all?"

"Don't," she said, her voice small. "Don't make it like that."

He interrupted her, not letting her finish, ignoring the hurt on her face. "Let me tell you what love is to me. A continual slog of violence. Blind optimism that propels you down the aisle of a church and then into making vows to people who are never going to do right by you. And I don't even mean just my wife. I mean *me*. You said it yourself. I was a bad husband."

"Not on the same level as your father," she argued. "Not like your wife was a bad wife."

He shrugged. "What did she get from me? Nothing but my money, clearly. And what about in your family? They're normal, and I think they might even be good people, and they still kind of mess you up."

"I guess you're right. Loving other people is never going to be simple, or easy. It's not a constant parade of happiness. Love moves. It shifts. It changes. Sometimes you give more, and sometimes you take more. Sometimes love hurts. And there's not a whole lot anyone can do about that. *But it's worth it.* That's what it comes down to for me. I know this might be a tough road, a hard one. But I also know that love is important. It matters."

"Why?" he asked, the question torn from the depths of his soul.

He wanted to understand.

On some level, he was desperate to figure out why she thought he was worth all this. This risk—sitting before him, literally naked, confessing her feelings, tearing her chest open and showing those vulnerable parts of herself. He wanted to understand why he merited such a risk.

When no one else in his life had ever felt the same.

"All my life I've had my sketch pad between myself and the world," she said. "And when it hasn't been my sketchbook it's been my accomplishments. What I've done for my family. I can hold out all these things and use them to justify my existence. But I don't have to do that with you. I don't think I really have to do it with my family, but it makes me feel safe. Makes me feel secure. I don't have to share all that much of myself, or risk all that much of myself. I can stand on higher ground and be impressive, perfect even. It's easy for people to be proud of me. The idea of doing something just for myself, the idea of doing something that might make someone judge me, or make someone reject me, is terrifying. When you live like I have, the great unknown is failure. You were never impressed with me. You wanted my architecture because it was a status symbol, and for no other reason."

"That isn't true. If I didn't like what you designed, I would never have contacted you."

"Still. It was different with you. At first, I thought it was because you were a stranger. I told myself being with you was like taking a class. Getting good at sex, I guess, with a qualified teacher. But it wasn't that. Ever. It was just you. Real chemistry with no explanation for it."

"Chemistry still isn't love, Faith," he said, his voice rough.

She ignored him. "I want to quit needing explanations about something magical happening. I wanted to be close to you without barriers. Without borders. No sketchbook, no accomplishments. You made me want something flawed and human inside myself that scared me before."

"The idea of some flawed existence is only a fantasy for people who've had it easy."

She frowned. "It's not a fantasy. The idea that

there is such a thing as perfect is the fantasy. Maybe it's the fantasy you have. But there is no perfect. And I've been scared to admit that."

Tucking her hair behind her ear, Faith moved to the edge of the bed and stood before continuing. "My life has been easy compared to yours. You made me realize how strong a person can be. I've never met someone like you. Someone who had to push through so much pain. You made yourself out of nothing. My family might come from humble beginnings, but it isn't the same. We had each other. We had support. You didn't have any of that.

"I don't want you to walk alone anymore, Levi. I want to walk with you. From where I'm sitting right now, that's the greatest accomplishment I could ever hope to have. To love and be loved by someone like you. To choose to walk our own path together."

"My path is set," he said, standing. "It has been set from the beginning."

He looked down at her, at her luminous face. Her eyes, which were full of so much hope.

So much foolish hope.

She didn't understand what she was begging him to do. He had thought of it earlier. That he could pull her inside and lock her in this cage with him.

And he might be content enough with that for a while, but eventually… Eventually she wouldn't be.

Because this hatred, this rage that lived inside him, was a life sentence.

Something he had been born with. Something he feared he would never be able to escape.

And asking Faith to live with him, asking Faith to live with what he was—that would be letting her serve a life sentence with him. And if anyone on this earth was innocent, it was her.

Even so, it was tempting.

He could embrace the monster completely and hold this woman captive. This woman who had gripped him, body and soul, and stolen his sense of self-preservation, stolen his sense of just *why* vengeance was so important.

It was all he had. It consumed him. It drove him.

Justice was the only thing that had gotten him through five years in prison. At first, wanting justice for his wife, and then, wanting it for himself.

Somewhere, in all of that, wanting justice had twisted into wanting revenge, but in his case it amounted to more or less the same. And he would not bring Faith into that world.

She stood there, a beacon of all he could not have. And still he wanted her. With all of him. With his every breath.

But he knew he could not have her.

Knew that he couldn't take what she would so freely give, because she had no idea what the repercussions would be.

He knew what it was to live in captivity.

And he would not wish the same on her.

He had to let her go.

"No," he said. "I don't love you."

"You don't love me?" The question was almost skeptical, and he certainly hadn't cowed her.

He had to make her understand what he was.

"No."

It was easy to say the word, because what was love? What did it mean? What did it mean beyond violence and betrayal, broken vows and everything else that had happened in his life? He had no evidence that love was real. That there was any value in it. And the closest he had ever come to believing was seeing Faith's bright, hopeful eyes as she looked up at him.

And he knew he didn't deserve that version of love.

No. If there was love, real love, and it was that pure, it didn't belong with him.

Faith should give that love to someone who deserved it. A man who had earned the right to have those eyes look at him like he was a man who actually had the hope of becoming new, better.

Levi was not that man.

"I can't love you. You or anyone."

"That isn't true. You have loved me for weeks now. In your every action, your every touch."

"I haven't."

"Levi…" She pressed her hand to his chest and he wanted to hold it there. "You changed me. How can you look at me and say that what we have isn't love?"

He moved her hand away. And took a step back.

"If there is love in this whole godforsaken world, little girl, it isn't for me. You'll go on and you'll find a man who's capable of it. Me? I've chosen vengeance.

And maybe you're right. Maybe there is another path I could walk on, but I'm not willing to do it."

She stared at him, and suddenly, a deep understanding filled her brown eyes. He was the one who felt naked now, though he was dressed and she was not. He felt like she could see him, straight to his soul, maybe deeper, even, than he had ever looked inside himself.

It was terrifying to be known like that.

The knowledge in Faith's eyes was deep and terrible. He wanted to turn away from it. Standing there, feeling like she was staring into the darkness in him, was a horror he had never experienced before.

"The bird is freedom. That's what it means," she said suddenly, like the sun had just risen and she could see clearly for the first time. She turned away from him, grabbing her sketchbook off the bed and holding it up in front of his face. "Look at this," she said. "I have the real plans on my computer, but look at these."

He flipped through the journal, until he found exactly what she was talking about. And he knew. The moment he saw it. He didn't need her to tell him.

It was a drawing of a house. An aerial view. And the way it was laid out it looked like folded wings. It wasn't shaped like a bird, not in the literal sense, but he felt it. Exactly what she had intended him to feel.

"I knew it was important to you, but I didn't know why. Freedom, Levi. You put it on your body, but you haven't accepted it with your soul."

"Faith…"

"You never left that prison," she said softly.

"I did," he said, his voice hard. "I left it and I'm standing right here."

"No," she responded. "You didn't. You're still in there." She curled her fingers into fists, angry tears filling her eyes. "That bitch got you a life sentence, Levi. But it was a wrongful sentence. The judge released you, but you haven't released yourself. You don't deserve to be in prison forever because of her."

"It's not just her," he said, his voice rough. "I imagined that if I changed my life, if I earned enough money, if I got married and got myself the right kind of house, that I would be free of the fate everyone in my life thought I was headed for. Don't you think every teacher I ever had thought I was going to be like my father? Don't you think every woman in Copper Ridge who agreed to go on a date with me was afraid I was secretly a wifebeater in training? They did. They all thought that's how I would end up. The one way people could never have imagined I would end up was rich. I did it to defy them. To define my own fate, but it was impossible. I still ended up in prison, Faith. That was my fate, no matter what I did. Was it her? Or was it me?"

"It's not you," she said. "It isn't."

"I can't say the same with such authority," he said.

"You're not a bad man," she said, her voice trembling. "You aren't. You're the best man I've ever known. But you can tattoo symbols of freedom on your skin all you want, it won't make a difference. Revenge is not going to set you free, Levi. Only hope can do that. Only love can do that. You have to let it. You have to let me."

He couldn't argue, because he knew it was true. Because he had known that if he brought her into his life then he would be consigning her to a prison sentence, too.

And if it was true for her, it was true for him.

He was in prison. But for him there would be no escape.

She could escape.

"For my part," he said, his voice flat, as flat as the beating of his heart in his ears, "I've chosen vengeance. And there's nothing you can do to stop it."

"Levi..." She blinked. "Can you just give us a chance? You don't have to tell me that you love me now. But can't you just—"

"No. We're done. The house is done, and so are we. It's already gone on too long, Faith, and the fact that I've made you cry is evidence of that."

"Please," she said. "I'll beg. I don't have any pride. I'm more than willing to fall into that virgin stereotype you are so afraid of," she reiterated. "Happily. Because there is no point to pride if I haven't got you."

He gritted his teeth and took a step forward, gripping her chin between his thumb and forefinger. "Now, you listen to me," he said. "There is every reason for you to have pride, Faith Grayson. Your life is going to go on without me. And when you meet the man who loves you the way you deserve to be loved, who can give you the life you should have, you'll understand. And you'll be grateful for your pride."

"I refuse to take a lecture on my feelings from a man who doesn't even believe in what I feel." She turned and began to collect her clothes. "I still want you to have my design. My house. Because when you're walking around in it, I want you to feel my love in those walls. And I want you to remember what you could have had." She blinked her eyes. "I designed it with so much care, Levi. To be sure that you never felt like you were locked in again. But you're going to feel like you're in prison. Whether you're inside or outside. Whether you're alone or with me or whether you're on the back of a horse or not. And it's a prison of your own making. You have to let go. You have to let go of all the hate you're carrying around. And then you might be surprised to find out how much love you can hold. If you decide to do that, please come and find me."

She dressed quietly, slowly, and without another word. Then she grabbed her sketchbook and turned and walked out of the bedroom.

He didn't go after her. He didn't move at all until he heard the front door shut, until he heard the engine of her car fire up.

He walked into the bathroom, bracing himself on the sink before looking up slowly at his reflection. The man he saw there…was a criminal.

A man who might not have committed a crime, but who had been hardened by years in jail. A man who had arguably been destined for that fate no matter which way he had walked in the world, because of his beginnings.

The man he saw there…was a man he hated more than he hated anyone.

His father. His ex-wife.

Anyone.

Levi looked down at the countertop again, and saw the cup by the sink where his toothbrush was. Where Faith's still was.

That damn toothbrush.

He picked up the cup and threw it across the bathroom, the glass shattering decisively, the toothbrushes scattering.

It was just a damn toothbrush. She was just a woman.

In the end, he would have exactly what he had set out to get.

And that was all a man like him could ever hope for.

Fifteen

Faith had no idea how she managed to walk into her parents' house. Had no idea how she managed to sit and eat dinner and look like a normal person. Force a smile. Carry on a conversation.

She had no idea how she managed to do any of it, and yet, she did.

She felt broken. Splintered and shattered inside, and like she might get cut on her own damaged pieces. But somehow, she had managed to sit there and smile and nod at appropriate times. Somehow, she had managed not to pick up her dinner plate and smash it on the table, to make it as broken as the rest of her.

She had managed not to yell at Joshua and Danielle, Poppy and Isaiah, Devlin and Mia, and even her own parents for being happy, functional couples.

She felt she deserved a medal for all those things, and yet she knew one wasn't coming.

When the meal was finished, her mother and Danielle and Poppy stayed in the kitchen, working on a cake recipe Danielle had been interested in learning how to bake for Joshua's birthday, while Devlin and her father went out to the garage so that Devlin could take a look under the hood of their father's truck.

And that left Faith corralled in the living room with Joshua and Isaiah.

"Poppy told me," Isaiah said, his voice firm and hard.

"She's a turncoat," Faith said, shaking her head. Of course, she had known her sister-in-law would tell. Faith had never expected confidentiality there, and she would never have asked for it. "Well, there's nothing to tell. Not anymore."

"What does that mean?" Joshua asked.

"Just what it sounds like. My personal relationship with Mr. Tucker is no more, the design phase has moved on to construction and he is now Jonathan Bear's problem, not mine. It's not a big deal." She waved a hand. "So now your optics should be a little clearer."

"I don't care about my optics, Faith," Joshua said, his expression contorted with anger. "I care about you. I care about you getting hurt."

"Well," she said, "I'm hurt. Oh, well. Everybody goes through it, I guess."

"That bastard," Joshua said. "He took advantage of you."

"Why do you think he took advantage of me? Because I'm young?" She stared at her brother, her expression pointed. "Because I was a virgin?" She glared at them both a little bit harder, and watched as their faces paled slightly and they exchanged glances. "People who live in glass towers cannot be throwing stones. And I think the two of you did a pretty phenomenal job of breaking your wives' hearts before things all worked out."

"That was different," Isaiah said.

"Oh, really?"

"Yes," Joshua said. "Different."

"Why?"

"Because," Joshua said simply, "we ended up with them."

"But they didn't know that you would end up together. Not when you broke things off with them."

"Do you think you're going to end up with him?" Isaiah asked.

"No," she said, feeling deflated as the words left her lips. "I don't. But you can't go posturing about me not knowing what I want, not knowing what I'm doing, when you both married women closer to my age than yours."

"Poppy is kind of in the middle," Isaiah said. "In fairness."

"No," Faith said, pointing a finger at him. "No *in fairness*. She was in love with you for a decade and you ignored her, and then you proposed a convenient marriage to her with absolutely no emotion involved at all. You don't get any kind of exception here."

He shrugged. "It was worth a shot."

"I don't need a lecture," she said softly. "And I don't need you to go beat him up."

"Are you still going ahead with the project?" Joshua asked. "Because you know, you don't have to do that."

"I do," she said. "I want to. I want to give him the house. I mean, for money, but I want him to have it."

"Well, he's the asshole who has to live in the house designed by his ex, I guess," Joshua said.

She sighed heavily. "I know what you're thinking—you're thinking that you were right, and you warned me. But you *weren't* right. Whatever you think happened between Levi and I, you're wrong."

"So he didn't defile you?" Joshua asked.

"No," Faith said, not backing down from the challenge in her brother's eyes. "He definitely did. But I love him. And I don't regret what happened. I can't. It was a mistake. But it was my mistake. And I needed to make it."

"Faith," Joshua said, "I know it seems like it sometimes, but I promise, you don't have to justify yourself to me. Tell us. I know what I said about optics, but that was before I realized… Hell," he said, "it was before I realized what was going on. I'm sorry that you got hurt."

"I'll survive," she said, feeling sadly like she might not.

"Faith," Isaiah said, her older brother looking uncharacteristically sympathetic. "Whatever happens," he said, "sometimes a person is too foolish to see what's right in front of them. Sometimes a man needs to be left on his own to fully understand what it was he had. Sometimes men who don't deserve love need it the most."

"Do you mean you?" she asked.

He looked at her, his eyes clear and focused. And full of more emotion than she was used to seeing on him. "Yes. And it would be hypocritical of me to accept the love I get from Poppy and think Levi doesn't deserve the chance to have it with you. Or maybe *deserve* is the wrong word. It's not about deserving. I don't deserve what I have. But I love her. With everything. And it took me a while to sort through that. The past gets in the way."

"That's our problem," she said. "There's just too much of the past."

"There's nothing you can do about that," Isaiah said. "The choice is his. The only question is…are you going to wait for him to figure it out?"

"I vote you don't," Joshua said. "Because you're too good for him."

"I vote you decide," Isaiah added, shooting a pointed look at Joshua. "Because you probably are too good for him. But sometimes when a woman is too good for a man, that means he'll love her a hell of a lot more than anyone else will." He cleared his throat. "From experience, I can tell you that if you're hard to love, when someone finally does love you, it's worth everything. Absolutely everything."

"You're not hard to love," she said.

"That's awfully nice of you to say, but I definitely

have my moments. I bet he does, too. And when he realizes what it is you're giving him? He'll know what a damn fool he was to have thrown it away."

"I still disagree," Joshua said.

"And who are you going to listen to about interpersonal relationships? Him or me?"

Faith looked over at Isaiah, her serious brother, her brother who had difficulty understanding people, connecting with people, but no difficulty at all loving his wife. She smiled, but didn't say anything. She felt broken. But Isaiah had given her hope. And she would hold on to that with everything she had.

Because without it… All that stretched before her was a future without Levi. And that made all her previous perfection seem like nothing much at all.

Sixteen

It had been two weeks since Levi had last seen Faith.

And in that time, ground had been broken on the new house, he'd had several intensive conversations with Jonathan Bear and he'd done one well-placed interview he knew would filter into his ex-wife's circles. He'd had the reporter come out to the house he was currently staying in, and the man had followed him on a trail ride while Levi had given his version of the story.

It had all gone well, the headline making national news easily, and possibly international news thanks to the internet, with several pictures of Levi and his horses. The animals somehow made him seem softer and more approachable.

And, of course, his alliance with Faith had only helped matters. Because she was a young woman and because the assumption was that she would have vetted him before working with him. What surprised him the most was the quote that had been included in the story from GrayBear Construction. Which, considering what Levi knew about the company, meant Faith's brother Joshua. It surprised him, because Joshua had spoken of Levi's character and their excitement about working on the project with him. On this chance for a new start.

For redemption.

Levi wasn't sure what the hell Faith had told her brother, but he was sure he didn't deserve the quote. Still, he was grateful for it.

Grateful was perhaps the wrong word.

He looked at the article, running his thumb over the part about his redemption.

And in his mind, he heard Faith's voice.

You never walked out of that prison.

She didn't understand. She couldn't.

But that didn't change the fact that he felt like he'd been breathing around a knife for the past two weeks. Faith—his Faith—had left a hole in his life he couldn't imagine would ever be filled. But that was…how it had to be.

He had his path, she had hers.

There was nothing to be done about it. His fate had been set long before he'd ever met her. And there was no changing it now.

He had gone out to the building site today, just to look around at everything. The groundwork was going well, as was the excavation over where he wanted to put the stables. She had been right about Jonathan Bear. He was the best.

Jonathan had assembled a crew in what seemed to be record time, especially considering that this particular project was so large. It looked like a small army working on the property. Jonathan was also quick and efficient at acquiring materials and speeding through permits and inspections. He also seemed to know every subcontractor in the state, and had gotten them out to bid right away.

Levi had already built on a property where money was no object, but this was somewhere beyond that.

He turned in a circle, watching all the commotion around him, then stopped and frowned when he saw a Mercedes coming up the drive. Bright red, sporty. Not a car that he recognized.

The car stopped, and he saw a woman inside, large sunglasses on her face, hair long and loose.

Flames licked at the edge of his gut as a sense of understanding began to dawn on him.

The blonde got out of the car, and that was when recognition hit him with full force.

Alicia.

His ex-wife.

She was wearing a tight black dress that looked ludicrous out here, and she at least had the good sense to wear a pair of pointed flats, rather than the spiked stilettos she usually favored. Still, the dress was tight, and it forced her entire body into a shimmy with each and every step as she walked over to meet him.

He'd loved her. For so many years. And then he'd hated her.

And now… His whole chest was full of Faith. His whole body. His whole soul. And he looked at Alicia and he didn't feel much of anything anymore.

"Are you really here?" he asked, not quite sure why those were the words that had come out of his mouth. But… It was damn incredulous. That she would dare show her face.

"I am," she said, looking down and back up at him, her blue eyes innocent and bright. "I wasn't sure you would be willing to see me if I called ahead. I took a chance, hoping I would find you here. All that publicity for your new build… It wasn't hard to find out where it was happening."

"You're either a very brave woman or a very stupid one."

She tilted her chin upward. "Or a woman with a concealed-carry permit."

Suddenly, the little black handbag she was carrying seemed a lot less innocuous.

"Did you come to shoot me?"

She lifted a shoulder. "No. But I'm not opposed to it."

"Why the hell do you have the right to be angry at me?"

"I'm not here to be angry at you," she said. "But I didn't know how you would receive me, so self-defense was definitely on my mind."

He shook his head. "I never laid a hand on you. I never gave you a reason to think you would have to protect yourself around me. Any fear you feel standing in front of me? That's all on you."

"Maybe," she said. "I didn't really mean for them to think you killed me."

"Didn't you? You knew I went to prison. Hell, babe, you siphoned money off me for a couple of years to fund the lifestyle you knew you wanted to live out in the French Riviera, and you only got back on police radar when you had to dip into my funds. So I'd say you knew exactly what you were doing."

"Yes, Levi, I meant to steal money from you. But I didn't want you to go to jail. I wanted to disappear. And I needed the money to live how I wanted. When you got arrested, I didn't know what to do. At that point, there was such a circus around my disappearance that I couldn't come back."

"Oh, no, of course not."

"People like us, we have to look out for ourselves."

"I looked out for you," he said. "You were mine for twelve years, and even when I was in prison it was only you, so, for me, it was seventeen years of you being mine, Alicia. I worried about you. Cared for you. Loved you."

"I'm sorry," she said.

"You're sorry? I spent five years in prison and had my entire reputation destroyed, and you're sorry."

"I want you back." She shook her head. "I know it sounds insane. But I… I'm miserable."

"You're broke," he spat. "And you're afraid of what I'm going to do."

The way she looked up at him, the slight flash

of anger in her eyes before it was replaced by that dewy innocence, told him he was definitely on the right track. "I don't have money, I'm not going to lie to you."

"And yet, that's a nice car."

She shrugged. "I have what I have. I can hardly be left without a vehicle. And I was your wife for all that time, you're right. And that's basically all I was, Levi. I enhanced your image, but being your wife didn't help me figure out a way to earn the kind of money you did, and now no one will touch me with a ten-foot pole. My reputation is completely destroyed."

"Forgive me for not being overly concerned that you faking your death has left you without a lot of options."

"In fairness, I didn't fake my death. I disappeared. That the police thought I was dead is hardly my fault."

"Alicia, are you honestly telling me you thought I would say I wanted you back?"

"Why not? You want a redemption story, and getting back with me would benefit us both. I don't think either of us were ever head over heels in love with each other. We both wanted things from the other. And you know it. Don't go getting on your high horse now. We can come back. You don't need to be vindictive," she said.

"I don't need to be vindictive?" He shook his head. "This, from you?"

She was standing in front of him, imploring him

to rescue her. That was what she wanted. For him to reach down to lift her out of this hell of her own making.

It was this exact moment when he knew he had her under his heel. He could take her in, make her think he was going along with her plan and maybe get some information about what exactly she had done that was illegal, and get the exact kind of revenge he wanted. Or, if not that, he could finish it now, devastate her.

And then what?

That question echoed inside him, hollow and miserable.

Then what?

What was on the other side of it? What was feeding all that anger, all that hatred?

Where was the freedom? Where was the reward? Nothing but an empty house filled with reminders of Faith, but without the woman herself inside it.

Somehow, he had a vision of himself standing by a jail cell holding a key. And he knew that whatever he decided to do next was the deciding factor. Did he unlock the door and walk out, or did he throw the keys so far away from himself he would never be able to reach them again?

Faith was right.

He had been given a life sentence, but he didn't have to submit to it.

Faith.

He had been looking for satisfaction in this. Had been looking for satisfaction in revenge. In hatred.

And maybe there was satisfaction there. Something twisted and dirty, the kind of satisfaction his father would have certainly enjoyed.

But there was another choice. There was another path.

It was hope.

It was love.

But a man couldn't straddle two paths.

He had to choose. He had to choose hope over darkness, love over hate.

And right now, with dark satisfaction so close at hand, it was difficult. But on the other side…

Faith could be on the other side.

If he was strong enough to turn away from this now, Faith was on the other side.

"Go away," he said, his heart thundering heavily, adrenaline pulsing through his veins.

"What?"

"I don't ever want to see you again. I'm going to write you a check. Not for a whole lot of money, but for some. Trade in your car, for God's sake. Don't be an idiot. I'm not giving you money for *you*, I'm doing it for me. To clear this. Let it go. Whatever you think I did to you… Whatever you really wanted to do to me… It doesn't matter. Not anymore. We are done. And after you cash that check I want you to never even speak my name again. Do you understand me?"

"I don't want a check," she said, taking a step forward, wrapping her hands around his shirt. "I want you."

He jerked her hands off him, his lip curling. "You don't. You don't want me. And I sure as hell don't want you. But I'm also not going to let you suffer for the rest of your life. Do you know why not? Because everything in me, every natural thing in me, *wants* to. Wants to make you regret everything you've ever done, wants to make you regret you ever heard my name. But I won't do it. I won't let that part of myself win. Because I met a woman. And I love her. I love her, Alicia. You don't even know about the kind of love I found with her. The kind of love she has for me. I don't deserve it. Dammit, I have to try to be the kind of man that deserves it. So I want you to walk away from me. Because I'm choosing to let you go. I'm choosing to get on a different road.

"Don't you dare follow me."

"Levi…"

"Leave now, and you get your money. But if you don't…"

She stared at him. For a long time. As if he might change his mind. As if she had some kind of power over him. She didn't. Not over any part of him. Not his anger. Not his love. Not his future.

It was over, all of it. Her hold on him. The hold his childhood had over him.

Because love was stronger.

Faith was stronger.

"Okay," she said, finally. "I'll go."

"Good."

He watched her, unmoving, as she got back in her

Mercedes and drove away. And as she did, he looked up into the sky and saw a bird flying overhead.

Free.

He was free.

Whatever happened next, Faith had given him that freedom.

But he wanted her to share it with him. More than his next breath, more than anything else.

He'd lived a life marked by anger. A life marked by greed. He'd been saddled with the consequences of the poison that lived inside other people, and he'd taken that same poison and let it grow and fester inside him.

But he was done with that now.

He was through letting the darkness win.

He was ready. He was finally ready to walk out of that cell and into freedom.

With Faith.

Seventeen

It was Sunday again. It had a tendency to roll around with alarming regularity. Which was massively annoying for Faith because it was getting harder and harder to put on a brave face in front of her family.

Although, how brave her face was—that was up for debate.

Her brothers already knew exactly what had happened, and by extension so did their wives. And even though she hadn't spoken to her parents about it at all, she suspected they knew. Well, her mother had picked up on her attachment to Levi right away, so why wouldn't she have this figured out as well?

Faith sighed heavily and looked down at her pot roast. She just wasn't feeling up to it. You would think that after two weeks things would start to feel better. Instead, if anything, they were getting worse.

How was that supposed to work? Shouldn't time be healing?

Instead she was reminded that she had a lot more time without him stretching in front of her. And she didn't want that. No. She didn't.

She wished she could have him. She wished it more than anything.

The problem was, Joshua was right. She was kind of secretly hoping things would work out. That he would come back to her.

But he hadn't.

That was the problem, she supposed, about never having had a real heartbreak before.

She hadn't had all that hope knocked out of her yet.

Well, maybe this would be the thing that did it.

Not at all a cheering thought.

There was a knock on the door, and her parents looked around the table, as if counting everybody in attendance. Everyone was there. From Devlin on down to baby Riley.

"I wonder who that could be," her mother said.

"I'll check," said her father as he stood and walked out of the dining room, heading toward the entryway.

For some reason, Faith kept watch after him. For some reason, she couldn't look away, her entire body filled with tension.

Because she knew. Part of her knew.

When her father returned a moment later, Faith knew. Because there he was.

Levi.

Levi Tucker, large and hard and absurd, standing in the middle of her parents' cozy dining room. It seemed…beyond belief. And yet, there he was.

"This young man says he's here to see you, Faith," her father said.

As if on cue, all three of her brothers stood, their heights matching Levi's. And none of them looked very happy.

"If he wants to see Faith, he might need to talk to us first," Devlin said.

Those rat bastards. She hadn't told Devlin. That meant clearly they'd had some kind of older-brother summit and had come to an agreement on whether or not they would smash Levi's face if he showed up. And obviously, they had decided that they would.

"I can talk to him," Faith said.

Their father now looked completely concerned, like maybe he should be standing with his sons on this one.

But her mother stood also, her tone soft but firm. "If Faith would like a chance to speak to this gentleman, then I expect we should allow it."

Her sons, large, burly alpha males themselves, did exactly as their mother asked.

"I'll just be a minute," Faith said as she slipped around the table, worked her way behind all the chairs and met Levi in the doorway.

"Hi," she said.

"Why don't we go into the living room?" he asked.

"Okay."

They walked out into the living room, where his presence was no less absurd. Where, in fact, he looked even more ridiculous standing on the hand-braided rug that her grandmother had made years ago, next to the threadbare sofa where she had grown up watching cartoons.

She had known she wouldn't be able to bring this man home with her.

He had followed her home, anyway.

"Is everything all right with the design?" she asked, crossing her arms to make a shield over her heart. As if she could ever hope to protect it from him.

As if there were any unbroken pieces that remained.

He tipped back his hat, his mouth set into a grim line. "If I needed to talk to you about your design work I would have come to the office."

"Well, you might have made less of a scene if you would have come to the office."

"I also would have had to wait. Until Monday. And I couldn't wait." He took off his hat and set it on the side table by the couch. And now she'd think of his hat there every time she looked at it.

This was the real reason he should never have come to her parents' house.

She'd never be in it again without thinking of him, and how fair was that? She'd grown up in this house. And Levi had erased eighteen years of memories without him here in one fell swoop.

He sighed heavily. "It took some time, but I got my thoughts sorted out. And I needed to see you right away."

"Yes?" She tightened her crossed arms and looked

up at him. But this time she didn't let herself get blinded by all that rugged beauty. This time she looked at him. Really looked.

He looked…exhausted. His handsome face seemed to have deeper lines etched into the grooves by his mouth, by his eyes, and he looked like he hadn't been sleeping.

"Alicia came to see me," he said.

Her stomach hollowed out, sinking down to her toes. "What?"

"Alicia. She came to see me. She wanted us to get back together."

Faith's response was quick and unexpected. "How dare she? What was she thinking?" Even angry at him, that enraged her. The idea of that woman daring to show her face filled Faith with righteous fury. How dare Alicia speak to him with anything other than a humble apology as she walked across broken glass to get to him?

And if there had been broken glass he would have mentioned it.

"It was a perfect opportunity to find a way to make her pay for what she did to me, Faith. She handed herself to me. Told me her troubles. Told me she needed me to fix them. I wanted to destroy her, and she handed herself to me. Gave me all the tools to do that."

Ice seemed to fill her veins as he spoke those words. Those cold, terrifying words.

What had he done? What would he do?

"But you're right," he continued, his voice rough. "You were right all this time."

"About?" She pressed her hand to her chest, trying to calm her heart.

"I do have a choice. I have a choice about what kind of man I want to be, and about whether or not I choose to live my life in prison. I have a choice about what path I want to walk. I was worried I was on the same road as my father. That his kind of end was inevitable for me, but it was only ever inevitable if I embraced the hatred inside myself instead of the love. You showed me that. You taught me that. You gave me…something I didn't deserve, Faith. You believed in me when no one else did. When no one else ever had. You gave me a reason to believe I can have a different future. You gave me a reason to want a different future."

"I don't know how," she said. "I don't know how I could—"

"Sometimes looking at someone and seeing trust in their eyes changes everything. You looked at me and saw someone completely different than anyone else saw. I want to be that man. For you. The man you see. The man you care about. That you want."

"Levi, you are. You always were."

"No," he said, the denial rough on his lips. "No, I wasn't. Because I was too consumed with other things. You are right. To take hold of something as valuable as love there are other things that need to be set down. Because love is too precious to handle without care. It's far too precious to carry in the same arms as hate, as anger. I couldn't hate Alicia with the passion that I did and also give you the love you deserve. It would have been like locking you in a prison cell with me, and you don't deserve that, Faith. You deserve so much more. You deserve everything." He took a deep breath. "I love you. I gave Alicia money. And it took the past couple of days to get that squared away. But I also drafted some legal documents. And she is not going to ever approach us. She's not speaking about me in the media. Nothing. If she does, she's going to have to return what I gave her."

"Why?" Faith asked. "Why did you…give her money?"

"To make sure she stayed out of our lives. I don't ever want her touching you."

"You didn't have to do that, Levi…"

"I would do anything to protect you," he said. "And I don't trust her. I needed to at least hold some kind of card to keep her away from us. And I knew that if she was just out there, desperate and grasping, she could become a problem later."

"But to give money to a woman you hate…"

He shook his head. "You know, suddenly it didn't matter as much. Not when there is a woman I love. A woman I would die for. Laying all my anger down was a small thing when I realized I'd lay my life down for you just as easily."

"Levi…"

"That feeling, *this* feeling," he said, taking a step toward her and grabbing her hand, placing her palm flat on his chest. "It is so much bigger than hate.

That's what I want. I don't want to be my father's son. I don't want to be my ex-wife's victim. I want to be your husband."

"Yes," Faith said, her heart soaring. Her arms went around his neck and she kissed him. Kissed him like she wasn't in her parents' living room. Like he wasn't absurd, and they weren't a ridiculous couple.

She kissed him like he was everything.

Because he was.

"What about your plan? I didn't think you were going to get married until you were at least thirty-five? And to be clear, Faith, I would wait for you. I would. I will. Whatever you need."

She shook her head. "I don't want to wait. I don't see why I can't have all my dreams. I'm an overachiever, after all."

"Yes, you are." He laughed and picked her up off the floor. "Yes, you are."

She heard a throat clear, and she turned, seeing her dad standing in the doorway. "I expected that the man who would ask my daughter to marry him would ask for my permission first."

Levi squared his shoulders, moved forward and extended his hand. "I'm Levi Tucker," he said. "I would like to marry your daughter. But, no disrespect, sir, she's already said yes. And strictly speaking, hers is the answer I need."

Her father smiled slowly, and shook Levi's hand. "That is correct. And I think…you just might be the one who can handle her."

"Handle me?" Faith said, "I'm not *that* hard to handle."

"Not hard to handle," her dad said. "You are precious cargo. And I think he knows that."

"I do," Levi said. "She's the most important thing in my life."

"I'm not that important," she said.

"No, you only saved me. That's all."

"That's all," Faith said, smiling up at him.

"It's good he proposed," her father said. "Now I probably won't have to stop my sons from killing you. Probably."

Her dad turned and walked back into the dining room, leaving Levi and Faith alone together.

"How badly do I really have to worry about your brothers?"

She waved a hand. "You're probably fine."

"Probably?"

"Probably," she confirmed.

She looked up into his eyes, and her heart felt like it took flight. Like a bird.

Like freedom.

And as he gathered her up in his arms, held her close, she knew that for them that was love.

Redemption. Hope. Freedom.

Always.

Epilogue

When the house was finished, he carried her over the threshold.

"You're only supposed to do that with your wife," she pointed out.

"You're going to be my wife soon enough," Levi said, leaning in and kissing her, emotion flooding his chest.

"Just a couple of months now."

"It's going to be different," he said.

"What is?"

"Marriage. For me. When I got married the first time… It wasn't that I didn't care. I did. But I thought I could prove something with that marriage. She wasn't the important thing—I was. No matter what I told myself, it was more about proving something to me than it was about being a good husband to her. And that isn't what I want with you. I love you. I don't want to prove anything. I just want to be with you. I just want to make you happy."

"And I want to make you happy. I think if both of us are coming at our relationship from that angle, we're going to be okay."

He set her down in the empty space, and the two of them looked around. The joy in her eyes was unmistakable. The wonder.

"We're standing in a place you created. Does that amaze you?"

It amazed him. She amazed him. He'd thought of her as too innocent for him. Too young. Too a lot of things. But Faith Grayson was a force. Powerful, creative. Beautiful.

Perfect for him.

She ducked her head, color flooding her cheeks. "It kind of does. Even though I've made a lot of buildings now. I've never...made one for me."

"You did this for *me*. I never asked you if that bothered you."

"Why would it bother me?"

"We talked about this. You haven't had a chance to design your own house yet."

She looked down at her hands, and then back up at him, sincerity shining from her brown eyes. "You know, I've always thought a lot about homes. Of course I did. How could I not, in my line of work? But I always felt like home was the place where you grew up. I never thought any place could feel like home to me more than my parents' house. I took my first steps there. I cried over tests, I was stressed about college admissions in my little bed. I had every holiday, endless family discussions around the dinner table. I never thought any place, even if it was custom-built for me, could ever feel more like home than there. I was wrong, though."

"Oh?"

She took a step toward him, pressing her fingers to his chest. "This is home."

"We don't even have any furniture."

"Not the house." She stretched up on her toes and kissed him on the lips. "You. You're my home. Wherever you are. That's my home."

* * * * *

Read all the Copper Ridge novels from
New York Times *bestselling author*
Maisey Yates
and Harlequin Desire!

Take Me, Cowboy
Hold Me, Cowboy
Seduce Me, Cowboy
Claim Me, Cowboy
Want Me, Cowboy
Need Me, Cowboy

#2659 THAT NIGHT IN TEXAS
Texas Cattleman's Club: Houston • by Joss Wood
When an accident sends Vivian Donner to the hospital, Camden McNeal is shocked to find out he's her emergency contact—and the father of her child. As floodwaters rise, he brings his surprise family home, but will their desire last through a storm of secrets?

#2660 MARRIAGE AT ANY PRICE
The Masters of Texas • by Lauren Canan
Seth Masters needs a wife. Ally Kincaid wants her ranch back after his family's company took it from her. It's a paper marriage made in mutual distrust...and far too much sizzling attraction for it to end conveniently!

#2661 TEXAN FOR THE TAKING
Boone Brothers of Texas • by Charlene Sands
Drea McDonald is determined to honor her mother's memory even though it means working with Mason Boone, who was the first man to break her heart. But as old passions flare, can she resist the devil she knows?

#2662 TEMPTED BY SCANDAL
Dynasties: Secrets of the A-List • by Karen Booth
Matt Richmond is the perfect man for Nadia Gonzalez, except for one slight hitch—he's her boss! But when their passion is too strong to resist, it isn't long before a mysterious someone threatens to destroy everything she's worked for...

#2663 A CONTRACT SEDUCTION
Southern Secrets • by Janice Maynard
Jonathan Tarleton needs to marry Lisette to save his company. She's the only one he trusts. But in return, she wants one thing—a baby. With time running out, can their contract marriage survive their passion...and lead to an unexpected chance at love?

#2664 WANTED: BILLIONAIRE'S WIFE
by Susannah Erwin
When a major deal goes wrong, businessman Luke Dallas needs to hire a temporary wife. Danica Novak, an executive recruiter, agrees to play unconventional matchmaker—for the right price. But when no one measures up, is it because the perfect woman was at his side all along?

SPECIAL EXCERPT FROM

HQN™

Read on for a sneak peek at the new book in
New York Times *bestselling author Lori Foster's*
sizzling Road to Love series, Slow Ride!

"You live in a secluded paradise." Rain started, a light sprinkling that grew stronger in seconds until it lashed the car windows. The interior immediately fogged—probably from her accelerated breathing.

Jack smiled. "There are other houses." The wipers added a rhythmic thrum to the sound of the rainfall. "The mature trees make it seem more remote than it is." Rather than take the driveway to the front of the house, he pulled around back to a carport. "The garage is filled with tools, so Brodie helped me put up a shelter as a temporary place to park."

Ronnie was too busy removing her seat belt and looking at the incredible surroundings to pay much attention to where he parked—until he turned off the engine. Then the intoxicating feel of his attention enveloped her.

Her gaze shot to his. *Think of your future*, she told herself. *Think of how he'll screw up the job if he sticks around.*

He'd half turned to face her, one forearm draped over the wheel. After his gaze traced every feature of her face with almost tactile concentration, he murmured, "We'll wait here just a minute to see if the storm blows over."

Here, in this small space? With only a console, their warm breath and hunger between them?

Did the man think she was made of stone?

She swallowed heavily, already tempted beyond measure. A boom of thunder resonated in her chest, and she barely noticed, not with her gaze locked on his and the tension ramping up with every heartbeat.

Suddenly she knew. No matter what happened with the job, regardless of how he might irk her, she'd never again experience sexual chemistry this strong and she'd be a fool not to explore it.

She'd like to think she wasn't a fool.

"Jack…" The word emerged as a barely there whisper, a question, an admission. Yearning.

As if he understood, he shifted toward her, his eyes gone darker with intent. "One kiss, Ronnie. I need that."

God, she needed it more. Anticipation sizzling, heart swelling, she met him halfway over the console.

His mouth grazed her cheek so very softly, leaving a trail of heat along her jaw, her chin. "You have incredible skin."

Skin? Who cared about her skin? "Kiss me."

"Yes, ma'am." As his lips finally met hers in a bold, firm press, his hand, so incredibly large, cupped the base of her skull and angled her for a perfect fit.

Ronnie was instantly lost.

She didn't recall reaching for him, but suddenly her fingers were buried in his hair and she somehow hung over the center console.

They were no longer poised between the seats, two mouths meeting in neutral ground. She pressed him back in his seat as she took the kiss she wanted, the kiss she needed.

Whether she opened her mouth to invite his tongue, or his tongue forged the way, she didn't know and honestly didn't care, not with the heady taste of him making her want more, more, *more*.

Don't miss Lori Foster's Slow Ride, *available soon from HQN Books!*

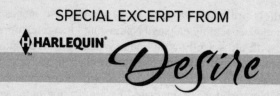
*Matt Richmond is the perfect man for Nadia Gonzalez,
except for one hitch—he's her boss! But when their
passion is too strong to resist, it isn't long before a
mysterious someone threatens to destroy everything
she's worked for…*

Read on for a sneak peek at
Tempted by Scandal *by Karen Booth!*

Nadia Gonzalez didn't believe in regrets. She simply did
her damnedest to never make a mistake. Being careful
but determined always paid off.

But there was a very good chance that Nadia had made
a mistake that put her job in jeopardy. She'd done the
unthinkable. She'd fallen into bed with her ridiculously
hot boss. A gaffe for the ages.

But the minute she saw Matt in a perfectly tailored
sleek black tux at the hospital fund-raiser last night,
looking unfairly handsome, she knew she was in trouble.
He almost never put on a tie. But as difficult as it was to
get Matt into a suit, it turned out that Nadia had a talent
for getting him out of it.

This was no small development in Nadia's life. She'd
spent the past fourteen months, virtually every moment
she'd been employed by Matt, secretly pining for him.
He was everything Nadia could ever want in a man, the
embodiment of sexy confidence, high IQ and seemingly

endless brilliance wrapped up in six feet two inches of the most appealing package Nadia could imagine, topped off with thick sandy-blond hair. When he walked into a room, men and women alike turned their heads. The air crackled with electricity. His mere arrival trumpeted his greatness, and was punctuated by his bracing blue eyes. Just thinking about him made her fingers and lips tingle.

Now, driving up a steep and winding hillside to The Opulence, an hour east of Seattle, her foot gunning the gas, these thoughts of Matt were ill-timed at best.

Yes, she'd wanted Matt for a long time and they'd shared an unbelievable night of passion. But so what? Was she really willing to throw away her career? No.

Was she willing to discount the years she'd scraped by so she could make a better life for herself and her family? Absolutely not.

Matt was not the settling-down type. There would be no happy ending with him. Which meant her first priority when speaking to him today would be to make sure he understood that last night was a onetime thing. They would both be better off if they forgot about it and returned to their strictly professional dynamic.

Even though that was going to break her heart.

Will they or won't they?

Don't miss what happens next!
Tempted by Scandal *by Karen Booth*

Available May 2019 wherever
Harlequin® Desire books and ebooks are sold.

www.Harlequin.com